WHITE HARBOUR WAR

WHITE HARBOUR WAR

A DANA VALKYRIE ADVENTURE

PETER M. BALL

GenrePunk Books (an imprint of Brain Jar Press)
PO Box 6687
Upper Mt Gravatt, QLD, 4122
Australia
Eclectic Projects: www.PeterMBall.com
Brain Jar Press: www.BrainJarPress.com

Cover Images: MMA Female Fighter © ArthurdidyK/Deposit Photos; Dark Futuristic Street Setting © GoodLightHunting/Deposit Photos; abstract splash © Eky Studio/Shutterstock.

ISBN: 978-1-922479-74-7 (Ebook) | 978-1-922479-75-4 (Paperback)

ONE

I got away from the *Viking Maiden* a little after 1600, sneaking off with the second wave of folks headed to shore for leave. Usually three days ashore had me looking for a fight, but White Harbor frowned on freelancers and didn't sanction pro fights on planet. It left me footloose and fancy-free in the prettiest water berth in the Boros Sector, with three days on my hands and instructions to avoid trouble. Pair me a crewmate, even Big Wade, my second, and I knew I'd find a scrap. Ergo, a prolonged solo R&R awaited me in the interest of obeying orders.

My plan involved putting distance between me and the docks, so I took the first left inland and cut under the high wall. Walked six blocks, going straight through Old Compton Way's twenty-four-hour party. The clubs and bars would stop the bulk of my comrades as they flowed ashore and engaged in the spacer's customary shore leave activities for time immemorial.

Big freighters dropped through the atmosphere above, casting long shadows as their approach blocked the sunset. The thrumming engine-noise dissipated as they approached, the seven-mile baffle walls erected between waterfront and city centre doing their job. Down on the streets folks laughed and smiled, hawkers urging me to step into the bars and. Drones flowed between the high, white-stone buildings, couriering small deliveries or keeping watch for the local SecDiv office. More security than I'd seen on any planet in a long time. Not a problem for an engineer on her best behavior. My plans involved a local luxury spa, downing a bloody steak, and collapsing into a soft bed where the tug of real gravity lulled me into sleep for the first time in an age.

For all I valued my status as Dana Valkyrie, the *Maiden*'s designated champ, White Harbor's too civilized for the rambunctious brawling and back-room fight arenas where talented spacers earned extra cash. As Captain Rackham reminded us in the minutes before we broke atmo, local ordinances came down hard on public brawling compared to most ports. Which is why I eschewed the free-flowing booze and heady pure oxygen tanks of Old Compton and made a beeline for the discrete, high-end baths and spas another four blocks over.

Halcyon Avenue is home to White Harbor's high-end entertainments, catering to wealthy locals and the occasional well-heeled spacer captain. I knew the prices precluded any but the most reckless spenders on the *Maiden*'s crew from following me this far inland, which should have spared me any unfortunate temptations.

But the universe moves in mysterious ways, and luck seldom favors those seeking the solace of solitude. As I angled towards my chosen venue—a smaller bathhouse tucked all snug and cosy into a narrow laneway off the Avenue—I spotted three familiar faces arguing with the white-smocked manager on the very threshold I'd hoped to pass through.

My steps faltered at the notion I'd need to share my favorite baths with three familiar faces, but I steeled myself as I caught the discussion's tenor. Two of the three, Birch and Hallahan, were weedy little featherweights who'd signed on the run before last, yokels from a backwater colony eager to see the bright spots of the 'verse. They'd fallen in with the third, Stig Jensen, not long after they'd come aboard. Regrets abounded now, given the way they backed off after Stig grabbed the manager's smock and raised a meaty fist.

I could have walked and left them to their fates, but the Captain named me the *Maiden*'s chief engineer and I felt some responsibility for her men. I closed the distance and put a restraining paw on Stig's wide, muscled shoulder and affected an innocent smile. "Well, then. What seems to be the problem here?"

Stig jerked his arm free of my grip. "Rack off, Valkyrie. This ain't nothing to do with you."

"If only we agreed," I said. "See, I think there're better uses for shore leave than keeping your ass out of trouble, but here you are raising a fist against a local with of a dozen drones fixing their cameras on you."

Stig released the merchant's smock and shrugged my hand away. The big fella weighed a hair over a hundred kilos, tall enough to loom over me when he bothered to stand up straight. He thought himself a hard man, throwback enough to resent a woman sitting atop the *Viking Maiden*'s heavyweight ranks. His eyes passed over me, gauging the odds if he took another crack at me.

I stared him down, and his shoulders sagged, anger leaching out of faster than a sponge wrung out over the sink. He changed his tactic, hoping to enlist my aid. "This asshole's trying to gouge us, Valk. Took our money, but he ain't willing to let us through the door."

I turned a raised eyebrow towards the merchant, who raised his hands in protest. "Our terms are explicit and stated upon booking: no tats, no trouble, no disrupting your fellow patrons. Your friend accosted a young lady on her way into the establishment, and she didn't feel safe bathing in the same facility."

That, I had no trouble believing, and both Birch and Hallahan adopted hang-dog expressions when I turned my attention towards the trio. "You hassling the locals, Jensen?"

"We're on leave. I'm having a little fun."

"Fun's when everybody's enjoying themselves. You're just bullying folks."

Stig Jensen firmed his jaw and his eyes blazed, but we both knew he couldn't whip me, even if he didn't want to admit as much out loud.

"Nuts to you, Valkyrie. You ain't in charge of nothing ashore."

It would have done my heart good to paste him one and bust

up Stig's ugly maw, but my brain knew it couldn't happen. "Way I see it, you've got two choices Stig. Option one, you accept your refund and find yourself another place to wash tonight. Some place yet to realize you're a pig who'll sully the scented water. You'll still have a job I three days' time, when the *Maiden* sets off for Khynal 8, and you don't drag your buddies into trouble they don't want."

Stig glanced over at the merchant, who paled and took a quick step backwards. I clicked my fingers, breaking through Stig's angry glare.

"Option two, you make an issue of this. I feel obliged to step in, so the *Maiden*'s not dragged into disrepute. SecDiv flags us all, and we get thrown in a cell. Lose our jobs when the *Maiden* sails without us."

"You think I can't beat you, Valkyrie?"

I held my tongue, because I knew the answer. I'd watched Stig train on the last few runs, knew he wanted to go ten rounds with the ship's champ. Size gave him an edge, but he fought using a boxer's stance. Nowhere near as adept on the ground as he should be, and too confident by half.

Stig raised his jaw and sniffed. "I got two men in my corner, Valkyrie."

"Maybe, but I'm thinking it won't matter. Win or lose, we're all in a cell, and you can't claim to be the *Maiden*'s champ if I don't work there either."

Stig's eyebrows dropped into a dour scowl. I sat back and let his ponderous brain assimilate my logic. Stig's not the brightest spark on the *Maiden*, but even he didn't relish finding another berth if the Captain set off without us. Few long-distance traders who visited Boros on the reg, and no real spacer signed with a short-haul vessel running the same system every trip.

His glare fell on the merchant. "Give us our money, ya berk. We'll have more fun some place without a stick up its ass."

The merchant sighed his relief and swiped a handheld to authorize the transfer. I stayed put until Stig checked his account and confirmed, grumbling all the while. The big lug stormed off down Halcyon Avenue, pushing his way through the locals.

Birch and Hallahan trailed after him, dust caught in a comet's tail.

The bath owner seized my hand and shook it, offering effusive thanks, and it was all I could do to calm him down and assure him it weren't no thing. I only asked he didn't hold my crew mates' behavior against me, given I planned on a good soak to relieve my aching muscles.

The owner—he introduced himself as Toby Haru—assured me I was welcome, and even offered me a discounted rate on his wares. I ain't so noble I turned him down. "I'll be off to grab some dinner first," I said. "Then I'll be back to take you up on that."

With my plans back on track despite Stig's efforts, I let the tension ease and daydreamed of the pleasures still awaiting me. For once, I would relax ashore, and do right by the Captain's reputation. It'd been too long since I'd had any shore leave where nobody expected me to fight.

This, I figured, would be three days to remember.

Some days I'm too damn prophetic for my own good.

TWO

The last time I'd landed on White Harbor, I'd found a small steakhouse named The Long Horn tucked away at the tail end of Moncrief Road. That was damn near two years ago, earth standard, and it pleased me to discover the little place had survived long enough to sample their fine medium-rare sirloins again. I followed the scent of cooking meat down a flight of stairs, turned into the restaurant tucked underneath a small antique shop.

I beelined for an empty booth up the rear, past the maze of diners and randomly paced tables. The whole place had a faint earthy smell, all wood and leather, serene as a distant moon. Just enough decor to make the place classy: white tablecloths, a spray of pinpoint lights along the ceiling, an inhibitor blocking AR signals to discourage terminal use. I felt alone for the first time since leaving the ship, despite sharing the space with thirty strangers and three servers. The clientele dressed better than I did, with far less scar tissue on their hands, but my credits spent just fine there, and the server took my order with a curt nod and a smile.

The proprietor ran the air conditioner, but kept the settings low, allowing White Harbor's languorous afternoon warmth to seep into your bones. A moment as close to heaven as I could imagine, and a damn fine salve after the encounter with Stig Larsen and his buddies. My steak arrived nine minutes after my scotch, a perfect medium-rare accompanied by steamed vegetables and thick-cut potato wedges. Food on the *Maiden* is better than most ships, but nobody who's spends time in the Black can escape the tyranny of preserved ingredients, fungal proteins, and soy. I lowered myself to the plate and took a deep whiff of the meat, savoring the moment.

My scotch went down cold, and I cut the first strip, mouth already watering. It took all my self-control not to wolf the meal down. The next three days spread out ahead of me, notable for the lack of demands. There were no engines needing my attention, no emergencies to handle. Nowhere I needed to be until my leave concluded. For the first time in months, I took my time and enjoyed my food.

Which is probably why it pissed me off when I caught the glare of an older guy sporting high-and-tight hair watching me from a nearby booth. A skinny fella, only five-eight, ears capable of picking up long-range comms jutting from both sides of his head. Ex-military, heading into SecDiv like plenty of 'em do. Off-duty, according to his jacket and collared shirt, but he made no bones about surveilling me. He wore small, circular glasses and an affable smile, his dark hair shot through with strands of grey. He carried himself like a former marine, which meant he knew *somebody* in my family.

Get into enough fights and you get a read on folks who mean you harm, and this fella's interest wasn't violent. He hadn't ordered a meal, just nursed a single glass and pretended he wasn't interested in moseying on over. I ignored his presence and concentrated on my meal. He'd either follow me, or he'd make his move, and I could bide my time.

He waited until I'd cleared my plate before collecting his glass and crossing the room. "My word, you're Dana Frampton, aren't you?"

My fingers curled into a fist just hearing the name said aloud, but I sucked a deep breath and steadied myself instead of hauling off and slugging him. My foolish decision to look over gave him an opening, and he seized it with gusto. "You are, aren't you? I recognize you from your mother's pictures. You used to write to her when we deployed together."

"That was a long time ago."

"The good old days," he said.

I bit down on the urge to stand and loom over him, maybe snarl a little. Irritating my mother's colleagues could only bring the old woman into my orbit once more, and I'd jumped ship on the *Viking Maiden* to get away from her.

The vet extended his hand. "Sergeant Edwin Fring."

I took it and held our hands steady when he attempted to twist his grip into the dominant position. "No offense, Fring, but I'm just here for a quiet drink."

He raised his hands. "Understood. Just wanted to say hello."

"Hello."

Fring hovered, waiting for an invitation to seat. I wasn't prepared to extend one.

"Listen," he said. "I know I'm intruding."

"Yes," I said. "You are."

"It's just, well, your mother. A friend, while we served, not just a commanding officer. Finest soldier I've ever known."

Fring eyed the bloody residue on my empty plate. "I know a little of your history. Your decision to skip a military career and sign-on with civilian transport. Your mother had a few choice words regarding your future that day."

"There would have been more if I'd gone through basic, and knocked out my CO."

"Your temperament is ill-suited to military life."

I raised an eyebrow, said nothing.

Fring retreated a step and raised both hands. "Your mother's words, not mine."

I've known enough SecDiv agents to recognize his overture as a preamble. "Can I help you with something, Fring?"

He took the question as an invitation and slid empty the empty seat. He produced and terminal and thumbed it to life, brought up video footage of me and Stig Larsen. He nudged it across the table. "Drone caught this earlier, and I recognized you. Figured, all things considered, I should give you a warning since you're new in town. Local governors have cracked down on fights over the last few years. No licenses issued for professional bouts, jail time for anyone caught engaging in an unlicensed fight. I hear rumors you're docked on the *Viking Maiden*. Ships got a rep and a half."

"I'm here to eat steak and enjoy the pull of gravity for a bit. I'm not looking for a fight."

It wasn't the answer he wanted to hear. Fring eased back and studied my face, trying to read something into the impassive stare and firm reluctance to engage with his bullshit. It wasn't surprising when he dug through his jacket and produced a vintage leather wallet, then flipped it open to show me his badge. "I work Security Division," he said.

"Old soldiers have gotta keep busy," I said.

"I'm trying to help here, Dana."

I bit down on my first response, counted to three as I drew a breath. Focused on the leathery warmth of The Long Horn, the fragrant scent of fresh-cooked steaks as the waiters hustled past, the clink of cutlery worked against plates just fragile enough to break if dropped 'em. Odds were, half the people in the place were locals who'd never worried about the impact of broken glass or ceramic dust getting sucked into a life-support filter.

White Harbor wasn't the place to charge at problems head-on, and resentment bloomed deep in my stomach. Fring reminded me of my mother in all the wrong ways, figured he knew me because they'd served.

In a fight, those assumptions get your ass beat. "I'm on a schedule, Agent Fring. And I've only got so much shore leave. How about we get to the part where you tell me what's on your mind and I get on with my evening?"

It caught him on the wrong foot, and for a second the smile dropped. He recovered fast, folding his wallet closed. "Just offering an unofficial warning. Don't let yourself get baited into throwing down. Spacers lose their berths when they're held for questioning and their ship's ready to depart."

"Must be a busy man," I said. "Giving unofficial warnings to every spacer who passes through here on leave."

The good humor drained out of his smile at the sarcasm, and I caught a glimpse of the man beneath. Hard, mean, and mission-focused, determined to win at all costs. I couldn't get a read on what he was trying to do, but odds were he felt duty-bound to my mother and thought I'd be grateful for his interference. He straightened his jacket and fixed me with a cold stare. "I'm trying to help you, Valkyrie. I'd rather not arrest you and screw with your career. Your mother would never let me hear the end of it, for one thing."

"My mother's seventeen systems from here."

"Eighteen, at the moment. I heard they redeployed her unit."

"Good news for me, then. And you needn't sweat my plans for shore leave. I'm not looking for a fight here, and I don't need no babysitter."

"With all due respect, Miss Valkyrie, you have a reputation. There are more citations for disorderly conduct in your file than a dozen other spacers combined, and your reputation says you enjoy brawling."

"I don't start fights, Agent Fring."

"Perhaps, but you don't avoid them, and you damn sure end them when you're so inclined. You take after your mother, there."

I'd kept up a pretty good guard through our talk, but that one caught me like a stinging jab brushing against your cheek. I set my jaw, warning Fring he'd touched a nerve. The white-knuckle grip on my drink confirmed it. In my younger days, I'd haul off and slug the man just to make a point, but my time on the *Viking Maiden* had tempered my fire a little. Taught me the value of picking my shots, and this wasn't one worth taking.

Still, Fring enjoyed seeing me riled. Knowing he could get to me. I wasn't going to let that stand, so I set my knife beside my plate and pushed the half-eaten meal away. "I think we're done here, Agent. I've enjoyed my steak, and it's time to find somewhere quiet to idle away the next few hours."

Agent Fring's polite, bland smile held a menace I couldn't quite place. "Make it a very quiet place, Valkyrie."

I abandoned the table and paid my bill, hit the street a riotous ball of anger in need of an outlet as soon as possible. Captain Rackham once told me an emotion's half-life is forty-five seconds. The hormones designed to trigger our fight-or-flight instincts burn out fast. If you're still feeling something strong after those ninety seconds are up, it's your brain pressing the button to trigger a fresh round of the emotion du jour. There may be some truth to her theory, but I fumed my way up the Long Horn's stairs and two blocks down the street.

I wanted to hit someone, preferably Agent Edwin Fring, but I knew a damn sight better than to sock the local SecDiv flunky in the jaw.

It took a lot of long, steady breaths and pavement beneath my feet before I got my anger under control, but I'll admit it's hard to stay furious on a street like Halcyon. White lanterns were strung between third and fourth floor windows, spluttering to life as the sun settled in the west. Humming drones floated overhead, merged with the jubilant merchant calls and the bathhouse scents at the Avenue's end. People dressed well and showered regular and wore their hair in elaborate styles, nothing like the sweaty, shaven-haired crew one looked at on a starship. Whatever else might have happened, I was footloose and fancy free for an extended break from *Maiden* life, and I chose not to dwell on SecDiv agents when a three-hour bathhouse soak still called my name.

THREE

I made it back to the bathhouse after sunset, right as the cool night settled over White Harbor. Bright, festive lights ran back-and-forth above the street, shedding soft illumination among the visitors below. A cool breeze came in off the docks, equal parts saltwater and the heady ozone from burning freighter engines, and the steel rod tension across my shoulders had me contemplating a massage. Toby Haru met me at the front door, as effusive in his thanks as he'd been when I departed, and I booked myself in for the works. One hour with the masseuse, getting rubbed down with sandalwood oils as the bathhouse systems pinpointed my knots; one hour soaking in the lavender scented bath, letting my aching muscles go loose and my troubles drift among the seaweed. I sprung for a canister of pristine, unstinted oxygen to enjoy while I luxuriated. Breathe in the recycled and scrubbed air every spacer takes as their lot, and there's no price too high for a little air untouched by other people's lungs. Toby Haru smiled and thanked me and took my credits, led me over to a small changing room with lockers against the wall. I punched in my code and disrobed, placing my hardware inside the small cubby and setting aside my coveralls and shirt for the spa to launder. Donning a fluffy robe, with a flower tucked behind my ear, I indulged in the glorious solitude.

My mother used to joke a spacer never relaxes, having spent

their life with one ear cocked for bulkhead leaks or life support hiccups. I can't say she's wrong, but I came damn close to real relaxation under the masseuses' ministrations and a hot water soak. For the first time in months, I closed my eyes and let myself breathe deep and happy. A smile ghosted my lips, and I debated whether living on a colony world had some merits after all. Might be I even feel asleep, or at least drowsed, given the startle when Toby Haru rapped a polite knock on my cubicle door.

"Ms. Valkyrie, I'm sorry to bother you, but your comm has been chiming for the last ten minutes."

I roused myself just enough to make an inarticulate, but clearly irritated, noise.

"I understand your position," Toby Haru said. "Ordinarily, I wouldn't have disturbed you, but it's a rather *confronting* sound."

I knew the sound. A harsh, aggressive siren the Valkyrie's onboard systems triggered for major malfunctions, designed to alert us to those air leaks and errors in life support my mother always joked about. The system had permission to break through all efforts to silence the comm, designed to be damn near impossible to ignore. No reason at all it should go off in a friendly atmosphere, which meant somebody had hacked the AI in order to make the call.

The crew with those skills is a short-list, enough to give me pause.

"Please, Ms Valkyrie." A wheedling tone in Haru's voice. No doubt my reluctance to leave a warm bath cost him any customers in the comm's range.

"Fine, I'm coming. Hold on a tic." I struggled free of the water and grabbed one of Haru's oversized towels, shoving my feet into the cotton slippers waiting beside the mat. I muttered dire curses as I burst through the door, leaving Haru to trail behind me as I beelined for the comm. A young couple at the counter raised their eyebrows at the exposed skin, or the years of scar tissue etched upon my body, but I ignored them and punched in my security code to retrieve the offending comm. The high-pitched wail set my teeth on edge and shattered any relaxation the bath had offered me, but I thumbed the device to life and set the console to 2D.

Big Wade's broad, handsome features filled the screen. Twenty-one and greener than the algae tanks oxygenating the *Maiden*'s atmosphere, but he proved himself an able assistant engineer and shared blood with the Captain. Once again, the damn kid proved too smart for his own good; he'd picked up how to hack our AI the first time I walked him through the systems, and he wasn't above using those skills in an emergency.

"You have two minutes to convince me I shouldn't kick your ass," I said. "Use them wisely, kid."

"Boss. I—" Wade's features creased, and he squinted at the screen. "Boss, you wearing a flower in your ear?"

"It's a hyacinth," I said. "You've got a minute-forty left."

"Right." Wade tore his eyes off the screen and cast a worried glance over his shoulder. The pitch and holler of a raucous crowd crackled through the comm, and I figured he'd picked a waterfront bar I truly wanted to avoid this stop. "Situation: Captain took us to this joint, The Angler's Loon. Captain's choice. Brought enough crew to fill half the room. She's been drinking heavy since we arrived."

"Cap can drink," I said. "Sixty seconds."

Sweat beaded on Wade's forehead, and he swallowed his nerves. "Cap ran into an old friend here. Woman named Lance. They've been goading one another. Placing bets. Boasting about their ships. Things are getting out of hand."

"How bad?"

"Dagash Four," Wade said.

I swore. Captain Rackham didn't drink to excess often, but when she did...well, I've known worse terrors. Not many, but a handful. Her bender on Dagash ended with her staking the *Maiden* on a drunken bet, and we'd come damn close to losing the ship. It took some quick thinking and faster fists to get us all off-planet with Rackham's ownership intact, and the Captain hadn't gone hard on the booze since.

I'd hoped she might have reformed for good, but I guess we weren't that lucky.

"Show me where things are at," I said, and Wade confirmed before turning the comm camera towards the commotion.

It never takes longer than a glance to recognize a spacer bar.

You walk into a joint and every patron has their hair clipped down to stubble, and it's a safe bet you've found the joint catering to short-term visitors. A bare head makes it easier to fit your skullcap and oxygen filters if you're headed into Zero-G, and it's one less thing for an opponent to grab when you're tussling.

If you can't peg the spacers by the hair, then here's your second hint: every spacer in the joint will be drunk, viciously loud, and determined to prove they're serving on the best ship in the port.

Wade panned the camera cross the crowd, then zoomed in. Captain Rackham sat at a scarred table, a glass of whisky at her elbow, her single good eye focused on a lean, blonde, hard-edged woman who sat opposite. I didn't recognize the Captain's drinking companion, but I recognized the expression on Rackham's face. Cool and calculating on the surface, but glossy with too much booze.

"How much as she had?"

"She's six drinks in," Wade said. "Placing bets with the other woman. Captain introduced her as an old friend. Owns a vessel docked across the bay. I've never heard of her before, but she's goading Cap something fierce."

I swore.

"Any other officers nearby?"

"Zadie stopped by for a drink, but she didn't stay," Wade said. "Tried to patch through on the emergency band, same as you, but your first port of call when the tech screws up."

"Roger that," I said. "Do what you can to keep your auntie from doing something stupid. Me or Zadie will be there to back you soon."

"Heard," Wade said. "I'll do what I can."

I closed the comm and swore, earning myself a wary glance from Toby Haru. I offered him my apologies and unearthed my clothes from the provided locker, getting dressed while still damp and covered in the water's lingering scent. As I dressed, I weighed the odds of wrangling the Captain on my own, given it would take a good half-hour to hoof it from the bathhouse to the Loon. Against my better judgement, I thumbed my comm to life and put in a call to Zadie Jayne, the *Maiden*'s first mate. Her irritated face filled my screen after the first tone. "There'd better be a damn good reason for this."

"Wade called. The Captain's getting drunk."

"This isn't news."

"She's getting drunk with a friend from the *old days*."

Few crew-members on the *Maiden* put in a longer tenure than me, but Zadie ranked among them. She recognized the threat the phrase implied.

"They still at the Loon?"

"Roger that."

"Shit. I'm a half-hour away. You?"

"Not much closer."

"Anyone there who can handle the Cap?"

"Wade, maybe, but he's already nervous. Hence the call to me."

Zadie shook her head. "I'll meet you there, and fingers crossed, she does nothing stupid before we arrive."

"Your lips to the Universe's ears." I pulled my jacket on and stumbled towards the counter, waving my credit chip at Toby. He scowled at the comm at my hand, but held his tongue as he processed my payment and thanked me for my patronage.

"Sorry to cut it short," I said, and wide-banded my comm code to his. "If Mister Jensen and his buddies give you any more trouble, please call me."

I barely caught his curt answer as I shot out the door, double-timing it down Halcyon Avenue with the comm clenched in my fist. I tried to keep myself from running, so I didn't attract undue attention, but even so I noticed two drones overhead, tracking my route through the city. Both unmarked, but I knew more than a few belonged to the SecDiv station, Agent Fring living up to his word to monitor me.

I hadn't planned on proving the asshole right and messing up, but all bets were off when it came to the Captain. I'd take the arrest, a conviction, and worse, to keep Captain Rackham from losing the *Maiden*. She wasn't family, but she mattered more to me than my own parents or any sibling.

And for all I didn't know squat about what she'd did with her life before she captained our ship, I knew enough to recognize scars, especially the ones most folks think no-one can see. The Captain didn't show hers often, but she needed back-up on the rare nights they were visible.

I prayed to all the gods in the verse Zadie or I would make it there before she did something foolish.

FOUR

I made it to the Angler's Loon in a little under twenty-six minutes, and even with my cardio regime, I breathed heavy with the effort. Big Wade met me out front, wringing his hands. He reported the same way I'd trained him to log engine problems, laying out the concerns and most recent steps to repair them. Thus far, attempts to cut the Captain off or remove her from the Loon were loudly rebuffed. Zadie Jayne arrived three minutes earlier and took a position at Rackham's side to curtail what she could.

"She's getting worse," Wade told me. "We're damn lucky she hasn't picked a fight."

"Captain walks with a crutch," I said. "Ain't going to be much of a fight, if it starts."

"You think being down a leg will stop her?"

I did not, but there weren't no percentage in saying it. Big Wade led me inside, using his bulk to forge a path through the dense crowd. The Angler's Loon proved to be a cramped, sweaty hole in the wall, deploying mirrored walls to give the illusion of space. Hotter than an engine room when the ships traveling at full slip speed and packed to the gills with spacers looking for a chance to cut loose.

I spotted Rackham the moment we entered, stiff-backed and perched at a table in the centre. Thirteen empty shot glasses lined up at her elbow, her good eye fixed on the blonde sitting opposite. If the Captain noticed the Loon's unseemly warmth, she didn't show it. Her huge black coat hung over her chair, her crutch resting against it, but she still wore the thick black sweater regarded as her uniform aboard the *Maiden*. I perspired the moment I stepped across the threshold, but sweat never touched the Captain's brow. Rackham might have been carved from ice.

As we approached, she raised a whisky shot in salute and tipped it down her throat. A roar went through the crowd gathered to watch the contest, and Rackham offered a sly smile as she added the empty shot glass to the line-up.

I spared a glance for her drinking companion and knew we were in trouble. An older woman, like the Captain, but she made concessions to the heat. She drank in a drab olive tank top, showing off powerful shoulders. This woman wore her hair long for a spacer, which meant little Zero-G work came her way and she felt no need to fit in with her crew. Age hadn't wearied her, but leant her features a craggy strength, like weathered stone standing resolute against the endless seasons.

A firm hand grabbed at my elbow, and Zadie Jayne fell in beside me. A slight woman, little more than a flyweight, but she could hold her own in a fight. "Captain Beatrice Lance," she said. "She owns the *Bester*, docked at berth 12-G. They worked together in the old days."

"Shit," I said, and meant it. The Captain said little regarding her life before stepping aboard the *Maiden*, but I'd been on her crew long enough to piece a few details together. She'd been military, fought in the uglier wars in her youth. Her tours hadn't been kind, and she bore no genuine pride in her accomplishments while in uniform.

I had no trouble believing Captain Beatrice Lance had served, based on the way she carried herself. Her long fingers curled around a fresh whisky, and she raised the glass to the Captain. "To the *Viking Maiden*," Lance said. "The second best ship docked on this planet."

Anticipation rippled through the crowd, and I'll admit, I could have walked over and taken a shot at Lance for the insult. There's few finer ships in any port than the *Viking Maiden*, and my engineering team worked dam hard to ensure she ran smooth as silk and faster than hiccup. To her credit, Captain Rackham didn't show her anger at the insult. A nerve ticked in the Captain's jaw, and she lined up her next shot before Lance's glass hit the table.

"To the *Bester*," Rackham said. "And her rag-tag, misfit crew who couldn't hold their own in a fight with a pacifist colony, let alone the well-trained crew of a *real* starship."

"Shit," Zadie said, and I echoed the sentiment. Those were fighting words in any spacer port you could mention. The Captain drank, and rolled the shot glass away from her mouth, never breaking eye contact with Lance.

Zadie and I double-timed it to the table, breaking through the onlookers waiting for the inevitable fight. We fell in beside the Captain, Zadie coming in on the Captain's blindside while I stood to her right, and we both adopted affable smiles to minimize the chances of things getting worse.

"Hey Cap," I bellowed, all bonhomie. "Making new friends?"

Captain Beatrice Lance broke eye contact with the Captain and fixed her stark, blue eyes on me. She scanned me, foot to forehead, and a tight smirk bloomed on her lips. "These yours, Aurelia?"

Captain Rackham didn't turn her head at all. "My first mate, Zadie Jane. My chief engineer, Dana Valkyrie."

"Pleasure," I said, and offered Lance my hand. The irritating smirk didn't budge as she took it and delivered a perfunctory shake.

"What do you fight at, Valkyrie?"

"One eighty-five, on a good day, but I ain't never backed down from a bigger opponent."

Lance closed her eyes and chewed her lip. "One of your strays then, Aurelia? Teaching her how to hold her own?"

"Valkyrie's the finest fighter you'll find on my ship or any other," Rackham said. "She could whip any sailor on the *Bester*'s crew, and she wins matches via knock-out."

Lance looked me over with a critical eye, unable to reconcile the Captain's words with the evidence before her. Her mistake. Despite her strength, I figured I could take her if a fight broke out. Beatrice Lance might verge on six foot when sober and capable of standing straight, but I still had two inches on her.

"*This* is your best?" Lance shoved a sneer into the question. "This is who you'd put up against Hockney?"

"It is," Rackham said. "Without a second thought."

"The man is a killer," Lance said. "I *made sure* he's a killer, Aurelia."

"And yet, I back my girl," Rackham said. "Today, tomorrow, and twice on Sundays, and I guarantee I'd walk away with your credits every time."

I won't lie: my chest glowed at Captain Rackham's praise, and it kept me from realizing how neatly I'd been set up.

"What do you say, Bea, you willing to take my bet?" Rackham said.

Lance turned to the crowd and barked an order. "Hockney, front and centre."

Bodies parted like the red sea to reveal the subject of her order. The way a fighter carries himself tells you a lot, and this fella carried himself like trouble. Hockney matched my height, gaunt for a light heavyweight, and he'd taken enough wallops to the mug to leave his features off-centre. Cauliflower ears from the friction of bodies of grappling on the mat, worn like a badge of honor. Long arms which blessed him with an impressive reach, always an advantage for a submission fella. I pegged him for a clean 190, one of nature's light heavyweights. There's no weigh-in for an unsanctioned fight, but it mattered. An extra pound or three, or a two inch reach, it all adds up. "Addison Hockney," he said, with a nod. "And you're Dana Valkyrie. I've heard of ya, lady, here and there. They say you knocked out Vic Dromos?"

"Twice," I said, no need to lie. "Tapped him once, too, on Turís IV, but he pretends it doesn't count because no officials witnessed him pounding the canvas."

Hockney chewed my boast over, then tipped his head at the *Bester*'s Captain. "Go ahead and make it happen," he said. "I look forward to choking her out."

"Finer folks than you have tried," I said. "Ain't no-one succeeded yet. But I promised the Captain I'd steer clear of donnybrooks, given the locals' attitudes towards public brawling."

"Bea and I have figured a workaround." The Captain produced hard copy currency, an affectation old timers cart around despite it being worth sweet fuck all. Rackham fixed Lance with a stony stare, fighting off a smile. "You call it, Bea. Heads or tails."

"Heads," Lance said, and the captain made the toss. The coin bounced twice on the tabletop and came to rest, a ruddy-cheeked face beaming up at us.

"Heads it is. We fight on *Bester*'s deck. Shall we say eight hours? I'll find us a referee?"

"Agreed," Lance said. "We'll see you there, *Aurelia*."

There are damn few folks who use the Captain's first name, and Lance dropped it freely. Captain Rackham didn't sell the familiarity, stayed perched on her seat, stiff-backed and refusing to give a damn inch despite the whisky in her system. She narrowed her one-eyed stare as Lance led Hockney into the cool night air outside and went off to prepare for the fight.

I stood beside her, giving away nothing, as the excitement of an upcoming fight waged war with the certain knowledge it would probably be my last as one of the Maiden's crew. SecDiv drones covered White Harbor, and Fring no doubt had me tagged as a person to watch.

FIVE

"For the record, I'm still against this," Zadie said. "Local prohibitions against fighting are ironclad, and nothing good will come of it."

We headed back to the *Viking Maiden*, Wade and I assisting a drunk Captain Rackham over White Harbors uneven cobblestones. The slow realization she'd had set me up dawned. Big Wade couldn't meet my eyes and I realized his distress call wasn't entirely spontaneous. Zadie assumed I'd be angry, and she wasn't wrong. Captain Rackham had taken me in and given me a home aboard the *Maiden*, taught me how to lead the engineering team and more than a few things about the fighting game I'd never have mastered without her help.

That she'd needed to trick me into showing up for a fight, rather than asking me to defend the *Maiden*'s honor, stung me and left me wondering whether I'd offended the old bird. The potential consequences of the bout, I'd decided, were best left until the fight was over. "What's done is done," I said. "I'm fighting now, and I'll need footage to scout Hockney's style."

Zadie dipped her head in acknowledgement. "You'll have it in an hour."

The Captain raised her head, and her stumbling steps threatened to drag Wade and me to the ground. "Shouldn't worry," she slurred at me. "Trained you. Know you're good."

"Appreciated, Cap."

"You can't lose to him, Valkyrie."

"Wasn't planning on it."

The Captain concealed her inebriation in the bar, but the booze hit her hard without an audience. Wade and I wrestled her into the *Maiden*'s galley and poured coffee down her throat, doing our best to sober her up while Zadie went to work.

Zadie is the Captain's right hand and a strawweight submission specialist in her own right. The woman you want scouting a guy like Hockney—she'd give me a run for my money if we both fought in the same weight, and against women her own size she could score the tap-out in under a minute. She reappeared after spending a half-hour on the search and ran the footage on the view-screen above the *Maiden*'s dining table.

"There's not much out there on the streams," she said. "Three authorized fights, two in the last two years, Earth standard. Emerged from nowhere at age fifty-three, with experience to make up the deficit against stronger, faster opponents. I'm running scans to pick up any enhancements, but I'm coming up with nada so far."

Big Wade folded his arms and firmed up his jaw. "So Dana's going in blind?"

He had damn near two feet on Zadie, but she didn't bat an eye at his scowl. "Not blind, just less informed than we'd like."

I poured myself a coffee and refilled the Captain's cup. Rackham eyed the liquid with suspicion, ignoring the screen. Me, I devoted myself to Zadie's footage, studying Hockney as he locked a wiry opponent in a guillotine choke. "He doesn't look like much," I said. "And it ain't like it's a tournament fight at all. Nothing but scratch on the line, yeah?"

Zadie and Wade exchanged a long glance which boded ill.

"Big chunk of credits riding on this fight." Captain Rackham's walking stick scraped against the floor, and she rose to stare at the screen. "Bea's a friend from the old days, and well connected. Odds are Hockney did unpleasant things, and they've assigned him to work below the radar after wrapping up his tour. He'll be more used to fighting for his life than taking home a purse. It'll be ugly."

The concern in her voice stung me, not least because she dropped me in the shit without warning. "You saying I can't beat him, boss-lady?"

Captain Rackham's smile quirked to one side. "My money's still on you, Valkyrie. I'm just asking you to take him seriously. Don't swagger in there assuming the fight's already won."

"I don't swagger."

"Course you do. Wouldn't be good in the ring if you didn't."

Zadie Jayne did her best to school her features, but I read worry in the faint hint of a scowl brushed across her face.

I cleared my throat and affected a confident smile. "How much you wagered on this one, Cap?"

"We won't lose the ship," Rackham said, and I'll admit I breathed a sigh of relief we'd got to her in time.

"She did wager our next run," Zadie said, and my relief faltered. "If Hockney beats you, the *Bester*'s hauling our cargo to Sirius Major."

The Captain's expression gave away nothing, but losing the Boros shipment would hurt. Truth is, the *Maiden* and freighters in her class operate pretty close to the bone. Drop one or two big shipments, and you're running at a loss. It's hard to keep a crew when you can't pay them for their work in the black, or keep the life support running clean.

I glanced Zadie's way, and her expression told me just how dire a loss could be in this fight. I couldn't figure why the Captain risked it, even in her cups. Rackham's always been a level-headed woman, and it ain't like she's never cautioned me against biting off more than I can chew before.

Wade, 'verse bless his cotton socks, didn't notice a damn thing. He scratched his wide, square chin and pondered the fight logistics. "We'll need an experienced ref if Hockney fights dirty. Cassie Majors and the Star Eagle splashed down a good hour back, and we might catch her and press her into service if we get our hustle on."

"Good instinct," The Captain said. "Track her down and issue an invitation. Let her know I'd consider it a personal favor."

Wade nodded, once. "And if she says no?"

"There's a man named Konstantin working at the Eagleton

shipyard. He owes me a few favors, and might be honest enough to call this one down the line when it comes to it."

Wade rose and disappeared up the ladder, getting started on the task. Captain Rackham eased her weight against the stick, scowling at the screen. "I'll corner you for this one, and Zadie will step in as your cutman. You're fighting for the ship's pride, so it's only fair the ship has your back on this."

Zadie cocked her head to one side. It had been years since the Captain elected to work a corner. "You're sure you're up for this, Cap? You hit the sauce pretty bad back there."

"I know how Beatrice thinks," Rackham said. "Odds are, Hockney thinks the same way. They trained with the same man back in the core, and he'll take his lead from Bea. You'll want me there."

Zadie flashed me a questioning look, and I shrugged my acceptance. On the screen, Hockney caught an opponent with a snap kick to the jaw, rattling him bad enough to shoot in, take him down, and fire off mounted punches. His style proved brutal and efficient, giving very little. My fight history gave him far more to work off, an opportunity to pull together a game plan tailored to my style. Every fighter brought habits to the ring, and a smart fighter studied and tailored their game plan to take advantage. I'd have to play things by ear, maybe try to rattle Hockney when his fight lasted past the first round.

It wasn't ideal, but I could work with it. Especially with the Captain sitting ringside, lending her eyes to the right and helping me work it out.

"Zadie, transfer what you've got to my comm," I said. "If I'm fighting tomorrow, I'll need some shut-eye and a chance to get my head right. Trust you can look after the Captain?"

"The Captain cares for herself," Rackham said.

"If she did it better, I'd still soaking in a bath before sleeping a comfortable hotel. Instead, I'm sacking out in my rack tonight."

"You love it," the Captain said.

"Not so much, right now."

SIX

Every fighter has their own favorite rituals before a fight. Some prefer a quiet dressing room, giving them time to run the game plan in their head before they head to the cage. Some folks deploy music to fire them up, get them pumped before they walk out and face the baying crowd. My preference ran to pretending the fight wasn't coming my way at all, doing everything I could to keep my mind off the impending violence in my future.

I racked up six straight hours of sleep and surfaced in the *Maiden*'s galley, hungry for breakfast. Captain Rackham beat me there, nursing a coffee as I strolled in. Her good eye was bloodshot now the buzz was over and the shots took their toll. Hangovers rattled the Captain worse than most. It's the closest we ever come to seeing her as human.

I poured the last of the coffee pot into a battered steel mug. "Feeling better?"

The Captain grunted.

"You know I'm not going to lose this one, not with the ship on the line."

"If I doubted, you wouldn't be fighting," Cap said. "But there's always the chance we're both wrong this time."

I snorted and made myself breakfast, a light porridge with salt and water. Something filling, yet not heavy enough to weight me down. I'd fought while hungry, drunk, and stuffed to the gills with chow, and I'd picked up victories every time, but necessity didn't equate to a preference. Against Hockney, I needed to be at my best. The champion of the *Viking Maiden*, ready to rumble when called upon.

"Captain?"

The word caught us both by surprise. Stig Rhoden loomed in the doorway to the mess, his chest bare and glistening in the dim light. He'd come without his buddies, returning to the *Maiden* solo.

"Cap, I heard a rumor you're sending Valkyrie to fight for the ship's honor. I'm thinking that's a mistake." He stepped into the mess hall, his eyes locked on mine, eager to be on with it. I'd butted heads with him a few times on our last crossing—Stig held potent feelings regarding his power and capabilities in the ring, and Cap allowed a match in the slip when she feared us coming to blows mid-journey. I'd weltered Stig good and proper in the South-West corridor for three rounds, and he'd gone down hard and crawled off liked a whipped dog who knew he'd met his match.

Some blokes get sense beat into 'em when they lose a fight, but others let it gnaw at them. The Captain rolled her good eye. "So what do you think we should do, Stig? Put you in instead?"

"Tha's 'zactly what I'm thinking."

"Last time you fought, she beat you, Stig. Clean and fair."

"That was then. This is now. We're on a world with gravity, and we both know I'm the better fighter when we're in a gravity well."

Cap snorted with annoyance and poured a fresh gin. "Fights in less than eight hours, Stig. I'm not thinking we should make a change at this late stage, do you?"

"I think a change is warranted, if it puts the right man in the fight." He lifted his chin and peered down his nose at me, head cocked to one side. A tough-guy pose, all challenge and cold malice. "Step aside, Valk. We both know I'm the man for the job this time."

Captain Rackham knocked back her gin, bristling and ready for trouble. She adjusted her grip on the crutch, her knuckles turning white. "Dana, we don't have time for this—"

"I'm thinking we make time." Stig Rhoden turned sideways and put up his dukes, adopting an old-school boxing guard. "Give me one round and I'll beat Valkyrie down, then show you all why ya need a real man as champ."

The Captain's nostril's flared wide, but Stig didn't read the warning signs. I stepped in before he could get himself fired.

"I ain't fighting you, Stig Rhoden. Not while you're drunk," I said.

"Ain't drunk—"

"You sure?" I asked him. "You were pretty steamed when I saw you last night. And, making a challenge to a shipmate hours before she fights for the *Maiden*'s offer? Talking down to the Captain? If you ain't drunk, you're all kinds of stupid."

"Ain't drunk," Stig Rhoden repeated. "My cousin pointed out—"

"Oh gods, your *cousin*," Captain Rackham said.

"Yeah, my cousin," Stig said. "He lives here, in White Market. Follows the fights on the streams an' all. She don't see why Valk is our champ at all. Way she sees it, Valk must have cheated me in order to pick up the win. No other way she outfights me, an' I'm going to prove it. You're going to fight me, Valkyrie."

I decided to short the fuse. I clambered to my feet, hands raised palms-out, like I wanted to placate the mug. "I knew you were dumb, Stig, but I didn't figure you were this dumb. How about—"

Stig darted forward with a wild bellow, unleashing a big haymaker which sped in like an asteroid strike. I sidestepped and tapped his ankle, let the momentum send him sprawling. Big fella hit the tiled floor chin-first, but it wasn't enough to knock him cold. Perhaps he was too dumb to stay down. He bounced to his feet and got his hands up again, came at me with range-finding jabs. Damn fool tried to connect with my jaw—fast way to mess up his hands, without gloves, and go into the fight with Hockney at a disadvantage. I got his rhythm and waited for the follow-up right, stepped under the swing and took the big galoot down. One hundred and twenty kilograms of angry spacer dropped to the floor, and I was on him in a moment. Three quick knees to the breadbasket softened him up, gave me room to bypass his guard and slap on an ugly chokehold. I cinched it tight and waited for the fight to go out of him, and it weren't long before Stig tapped.

Captain Rackham poured another gin and raised it in salute. "Don't see you bust out a submission often," she said.

"Didn't want to hurt my hands ahead of tussling with Hockney, and a drunk Stig's ain't going to stretch my submission game."

The Captain rose to her feet with a soft grunt, using the crutch to steady herself. She limped to the sink and filled a glass, splashed water over Stig's face to bring him back to the land of the living. The big fella fought his way through the fog. He muttered beneath his breath, stream-of-consciousness nonsense as he pieced together what had happened.

Captain Rackham nudged him with her boot. "Get yourself together and pack your gear," Rackham said. "I want you off this ship before the fight with Hockney's over."

Spacers are used to losing jobs, often for less than half the trouble Stig caused, in far less time. Usually they got out with a busted lip and the sure knowledge there's always more work for a decent hand, even if it takes a few weeks to find it. It seemed Stig Rhoden wanted to play things differently this time. He stared up at the Captain, panic setting in as the consequences seeped in.

"Aw, no," he said. "Please, you gotta let me fight for you. You gotta put me in against Hockney."

Captain Rackham raised an eyebrow. "I don't got to do nothing, Stir. You brought this on yourself. Maybe should have listened to another cousin, yes?"

Now hot tears spilled down Stig's fat cheeks. "You don't understand, Cap. I *need* to be in this fight. If Valk goes out there and whips this fella..."

"*When* I go out there and whip him," I said. "Ain't no doubt what's going to happen, Stig."

"You don't understand," Stir wailed. "My cousin... Mitch...she was counting on me. She needed me in the fight to ensure things went her way. My whole family's going to be ruined, Cap. You can toss me on my ass right after, but ya gotta let me fight."

Rackham and I exchanged a long look. This wasn't what we expected from Stig. The old woman still possessed the occasional soft spot. She returned to the table and poured another drink, motioned for Stig to start talking.

"My cousin, she owns a tea-house," Stig said. "Nice place, and peaceful-like. Best spot in the whole damn market if you're looking for a quiet time. An' she's being leaned on, a bad piece of work who owns the Tea House's debt. We needed to pay him back fast, and Mitch heard you were fighting and hatched herself a plan. Figured I could come in here and score the spot, make sure we knew the result and rig the fight."

"You lousy bastard," I said. "You wanted to walk in there and throw the fight!"

Stig's shoulders sagged, and he didn't meet our eyes. "Wasn't much of a plan, but Mitch is desperate," he said. "An' she figured I could take you. Hell, she already lay her bets... they'll wipe her out, if you—"

"When!" I said, my voice loud. Stig dipped his head low, expecting me to swat him. I didn't have the heart.

"When you win," he finished, shoulders drooping. "If he goes down, my kin goes down with him. You can't do it to us, Cap."

"I ain't putting you in a fight for a boat you don't work on," Captain Rackham said. "And I don't rightly think we owe much to you or your cousin, just because of the stupidity you've displayed in the last thirty minutes. But I've got no desire to see a family ruined, so put in a call and tell her the scheme is off."

"She won't trust a call," Stig said. "Mitch lives off the net when she can. Someone will need to tell her in person. If ya let me—"

"You ain't doing spit," the Captain said, "except clearing your bunk and getting off my boat." She turned on her heel and left, her crutch's steady click echoing down the corridor. Stig huddled on the floor, sniffling, pathetic as a sodden dog trying to get back into the house.

In any port but White Harbor, I wouldn't have felt for the lug. Stig Rhoden had proven himself a bad influence, thicker than a bulkhead yet able to pull folks into his orbit. While I don't hold a grudge against any fighter for taking their shot, fellas like Stig don't earn much sympathy either, and the Captain's decision to run him off the Maiden was the right call, and one I'd make myself.

But after being thrown in the deep end, and knowing I'd probably follow Stig out the door if my fight if SecDiv caught wind of the Hockney bout, I had a momentary pang for what I could lose and saw a little of myself in Stig Rhoden's tears.

Which is why, against my better judgement, I fell into offering to help him out.

"Tell you what, Stig, I got some free time before the fight," I said, "and I ain't one to hold a grudge. I can stop by your cousin's shop and tell her what's what. It ain't much, but she won't waste her money."

Stig eyebrows shot up. "You'd do that?"

"Sure. Where's she at?"

"The Lotus, on Hammersley Street," Stig said. "You can't miss it. Biggest tea shop you've ever seen."

Hammersley Street wasn't far from the docks. Easy to get to, and back, before the fight. One last favor to do right by a crewmate, even if he weren't my favorite.

"I'll get it done in a jiffy," I said. "Best you get to packing. The Captain ain't joking around about kicking you off."

SEVEN

I spent an hour traipsing up-and-down Hammersley Street without finding hide-nor-hair of The Lotus, and I don't mind saying my goodwill towards Stig Rhoden and his cousin faded a little more with each frustrating block I covered. In the end, I grabbed a well-dressed local and asked 'em if they could help me out, and they directed me two blocks over, on Halberg Avenue, where the Lotus moved four years back. I grumbled my way down a cross-street, cursing Stig for a blockhead, but once I found myself on Halberg, there was no missing the joint.

The Lotus perched on a busy intersection: three stories, old stone and white wood. The front wall replaced with big, tinted windows offering patrons on all three levels a view all the way down the sloping hill to the bustling harbor. Augmented reality ads assaulted me as I crossed the street, but I brushed them away. My comm chimed in my ear, a message on the *Maiden*'s channel.

"Valk, what in hell you doing?" Zadie Jayne asked. "Captains just realized you're off the ship."

"Captains' getting slow then," I said. "Just ducked out to do some business."

"Getting embroiled in Stig's drama isn't smart, Valk."

"Captain picked a fight on White Harbor," I said. "After giving us seven different warnings to stay out of trouble while we're dockside."

Zadie said nothing in response. We both knew fighting Hockney rated way up there on the list of bad ideas, but we'd both do it to preserve the Captain's pride. Both sides would take pains to keep SecDiv from discovering the bout, but surveillance drones and loose lips have ruined many a good fight night when things were organized fast.

"Listen, Zadie. I can't sit in the ship and brood over this. It'll take me, what, fifteen minutes to warn the kid his cousin's not in the ring tonight? I'll be on deck at the *Bester* with time in my pocket, if you're worried about whipping Hockney's ass."

"If you aren't free to take down Hockney, I'll take the asshole," Zadie said. "But the captain ain't happy, Valk."

"The Cap's a soft touch from way back," I said. "If I weren't here, she'd find some other way to get news to the Lotus."

I killed the command and shouldered my way inside. Cool air brushed against my cheek, rich with tannin scents and perfumes, a subtle hint of steam rising from every cup and teapot. A waiter strolled over, one eyebrow raised as she asked if I needed a seat.

"I'm looking for Mitch Rhoden," I said. "Hear tell he owns this joint."

The waiter ran his eyes down my frame and sniffed his distaste at my request, but he scurried off to the second story with a modicum of haste. A moment later, he tagged out to a skinny, bespectacled woman with a short, crimson bob and tasteful silver jewelry splashed across her fingers and throat. Her gown rustled like falling leaves and she deployed a smile best turned on patrons fancier and better behaved than a space-faring roughneck. "I'm Mitch Rhoden," she said, offering me a delicate hand. "A pleasure."

"Pleasure's all mine," I said. "Name's Valkyrie. Dana, to my friends. I worked with your cousin, Stig, on the *Viking Maiden*."

Mitch Rhoden didn't miss a trick. She looped one hand over my elbow and invited me to talk in her private office, guiding me up three flights of stairs and through the staff doors at the rear. We bypassed the small galley kitchen, the ornate décor giving way to plebeian concrete floors and sweat-stained staff working at speed.

Rhoden's office proved small and neat, with a tea set on the desk. She guided me into the visitor's seat.

"Tea?"

"I strike you as a tea drinker?"

"You strike me as a woman doing a favor for my idiot cousin."

I wasn't expecting that kind of insight from anyone related to Stig. "I never said anything about a favor."

"No, but you said 'worked', downstairs. I know Stig well enough to read between the lines." Mitch's head tilted to the left, and her eyes traced my face and shoulders. "You may not drink tea, but I promise you'll enjoy this one. It's one of our best, and I expect I'll owe you that much…"

I shrugged my ascent, and Mitch Rhoden went to work with her tea set, scooping dark leaves into the pot and ordering hot water from her kitchens. I sat quietly, watching the slight woman work, admiring the precision of her movements and the focus she brought to the task. She presented me with a fine, bone-China cup that felt too-small in my big mitts, then settled on the far side of the desk.

"So," she said. "Tell me what my cousin's done."

I took a deep breath and caught the scents of the tea. Hints of lavender and heady, pleasant tang I couldn't quite place. I might have taken a sip right then, but Mitch Rhoden's big-eyed stare waited for news, so I sighed and forged on with the details. "Stig tried to advance his career on the *Maiden* at an inopportune time," I said. "Right now, he's packing his gear and leaving Captain Rackham's crew. Clearing his bunk with take an hour, and the paperwork will take longer. Odds are, he'll be along after that, looking for a place to crash until he scores a new gig. He wanted me to give you a heads up he won't be facing the *Bester*'s champ tonight, and any side-bets you've got placed on the fight—"

"Valkyrie!" Mitch clicked her fingers, twigging to where she'd heard the name. "He claimed he'd take your place tonight."

"Not sure where he picked up that notion," I said. "Nobody represents the *Maiden* but me, in these matters."

"No. Of course, you're quite correct. Accept my apology,

please." Mitch fixed me with a reproachful look, biting her lower lip. She smoothed her apron with both hands, and flashed me a wan smile. "Tea," she said. "How is your tea?"

I slurped a mouthful, just to be polite, and then another because it tasted better than tea had any right to be. Half the cup disappeared while Mitch Rhoden regrouped. "This is good," I said. "Best tea I've had."

A faint blush touched Mitch Rhoden's cheeks, and her gaze slid towards her desktop. Nervous fingers twitched in her lap, and she ignored the steaming cup of tea at her own elbow. "I'm afraid I don't understand the inner workings of a ship's crew," she said. "How one person gets selected, and other is passed by. I'm so sorry if Stig overstepped his mark."

"It's fine," I said. "Didn't mean to be harsh. It's just…, I earned my spot as the ships champ, fair and square. Your cousin never came close to beating me, even on his best day. Wasn't smart, urging him to try and step up so close to a grudge match."

Mitch Rhoden's gaze snapped upright, shocked. Her laughter twinkled, beautiful as a distant star. "I never asked Stig to do anything so stupid," she said. "He mentioned the fight coming up tonight, and the hot bets some folks are placing. I made a stupid joke, how we could clean up if *he* repped your ship and controlled the outcome. Foolish talk, which triggered a long rant about you cheating him in your last bout—"

"Lies!" I said. "I beat him, fair and square."

"—and next thing I know, he's assuring me everything's in the bag. All I've got to do is place money on Hockney, and my money troubles will be over!"

"Here's hoping you didn't listen to him," I said, "'cause I'm still in the fight tonight, and I've got no intention of losing."

"Oh dear," Mitch said. "I hope Stig's not hurt."

"I went easy on him," I said, flashing a wolfish grin. "Pride will hurt more than anything else, but he's got a few bruises to lick while he figures out what to do next. Mostly, he's concerned you'll take a bath and lose your joint."

"No fear," Mitch said. "I'm not one for gambling—I'm not even sure where to place a bet on a fight. As useful as the money would be in paying down our debts, I've held off committing anything until Stig arrived to help."

"Well, I'm sure there's weight off his mind," I said. "Poor fella's convinced he ruined you, when he realized he'd bit off more than he could chew. This counts as good news, I'm thinking."

Mitch offered me a wan, uneasy smile and toyed with her apron hem. "Yes," she said. "Very good." A tear splashed onto her desktop, and she turned away from me.

"Aw, hell," I said. "You're in deep, ain't you? How much do you owe?"

"Too much," Mitch said. "Far too much to take a risk on what little I've got stashed away."

"You could still back me in the fight," I said. "Ain't certain, but there's damn few folks I ain't beat in any part of the verse, and I don't see nothing in Addison Hockney to convince me he's a threat."

My tongue ran loose and free in my mouth, and those words weren't any I'd say out loud under usual circumstances. Captain drills us hard on knowing our limits, and never promising anyone an easy win. Fights are unpredictable, and even the clumsiest puncher is in with a chance if they land a shot. But sitting there, amid the heady scents of the tea and the soft lilt of Mitch Rhoden's voice, I felt myself invincible as a drunkard and just as inclined to boast.

If Mitch Rhoden had credits to burn and an inclination to take a risk, I'd go out there and win her enough to secure her tea shop three times over.

Her eyes shone with sheer joy at the prospect, but even she knew enough to regard my assurances with suspicion. "I'm sure you're very good," she said. "Taking a fella Stig's size tells me you're no slouch in a brawl—but I don't know you and I don't know your opponent. It's just too much risk..."

Her voice trailed off, and I nodded. "Fair. You don't even know me by reputation."

"I don't suppose," she said in a small voice, "you'd consider doing a gal a favor and throwing the fight yourself? I'd split my winnings with you, once I've cleared the debts I've accumulated—"

"Darlin', even if you found me amenable to the idea," I said, "throwing a fight's not going to fly with me. You might need certainty, but the *Viking Maiden*'s crew will be turning out for this one. Thirty-three folks with money on my winning, including my Captain and my closest friends. I can't throw a fight when it'll cost them credit and pride alike, even if I'm feeling sorry for ya."

"Of course." Mitch hunched and studied her thumbs. "We'll find another way, I guess. More tea?"

I regarded my empty cup, unsure when I'd finished the brew. "Best not," I said, tongue growing thick in my mouth. "Don't want to go into the fight with a full stomach. Not great if they land a gut-punch."

Mitch Rhoden nodded primly and collected my cup. She set it aside, away from the silver tray and her own untouched tea cup. "Well, then," she said. "Good luck in your fight, Ms. Valkyrie."

I took my leave, planning to head back to the *Viking Maiden* and kill time before the fight. The first step told me I was in trouble, unsteady on my feet. I got halfway down the first flight of stairs before my head went woozy, and I clutched at the banister as my balance went off-kilter and threatened to send me tumbling to the floor. I held tight, trying to breathe and clear my vision, but the damn room spun a waltz around me and the floor came up to give me a drunkard's kiss.

I hit hard, like a fighter who's been poleaxed and can't even keep their feet no more, and as the darkness rushed in I heard footsteps and someone complaining I was a big 'un.

I wanted to fire back, with words or with punches, but I don't know I got either out before the darkness claimed me.

EIGHT

I came to in a cramped, dusty storeroom with my arms and feet taped to a chair, the light streaming in from a grubby windowpane set high in the wall. Musty tea scents everywhere, and every box on the shelves bore names like "Earl Grey Blend" and "Martian Rooibos". My head swam with the lingering effects of whatever I'd been given, alternating between sharp pain and nausea-inducing fuzzy vision. If I'd been drinking, the heavy, hung-over feeling wouldn't have bothered me none. As I'd drunk nothing stronger than Mitch Rhoden's special blend, and I weren't inclined to keel over and pass out after tea, I surmised she'd slipped me a micky after filling my cup. They'd taken my comm, and my shoes, and their tape-job had been a little too tight. Pins and needles plagued my left hand, and it hurt to curl my toes. I couldn't tell how long I'd been out, but the dirty sunlight suggested we'd moved into the afternoon hours and the fight drew closer, and they hadn't taken me far.

The creeping realization I'd been suckered crept over me and hurt worse than the bumps I'd taken collapsing on the stairwell. Whatever they'd used to drug me hit hard, and its after-effects left me queasy and hurting. Probably figured they'd take me out of the fight, and clean up betting on the forfeit or Hockney beating whichever second the Captain put into the cage in my place. Odds are, I'd keep my spot on the crew, but the prospect held little pleasure knowing what the Captain would lose on the fight.

I drew a deep breath and focused on blocking the pain, the first step in breaking free. I could see three walls from my bound position, which suggested they'd positioned me facing away from the door. My chair creaked beneath my weight, but the sounds behind me interested me more. The thin whistle of someone with an oft-broken nose trying to breathe normally. The soft rasp of old-fashioned playing cards being shuffled, arranged, and played. They'd left someone to stand guard over me, and probably more than one.

They hadn't bothered gagging me, but I kept my trap shut. Attempting to twist and stare at the door merely sent my head lolling to one side, my neck not quite up to the job of holding my skull upright. I tested the tape around my wrists and ankles, twisting rather than pulling free to minimize the odds of drawing attention. They'd invested in some high-quality gear, damn near impossible to split. I curled my fingers over the chair's arm, holding back a few choice curses.

"She's awake," one of my captors said, and his chair scraped against the concrete floor a second before he stepped into view. A big bruiser, bulky with muscle, who wore a jaunty little hat with an orange feather in the brim. I did my best to feign unconsciousness, but as an actor, I make a damn good fighter.

Jaunty Hat crouched down to get on my level. "Hello, Princess. Welcome back to the land of the living."

"Could use a drink," I mumbled, and Jaunty Hat laughed.

"I'm betting."

"We had to tranque you pretty hard, you being a big lass and all." The second voice boomed from a space behind my head, and I winced at the volume.

Jaunty Hat rolled his eyes. "She doesn't need to know, dim bulb."

"I'm just making conversation here."

"The job isn't talking to her. It's keeping her here, all trussed up like a ham."

"Still need water," I croaked. "'Less you enjoy cleaning up vomit."

Jaunty Hat's eyes locked on somebody around me, an entire conversation put into the stare. His companion smiled, and another chair scraped backwards.

"Fine," the other fella said. "I'll get her water."

A minor victory, but an important one. I've never been a soldier, but I'd picked up a few things to try when you're captured by the enemy. Separating their numbers is a top priority, and it didn't hurt I really needed a refreshing liquid to clear my head.

"You should get comfy," Jaunty Hat said. "You're going to be here for another six hours."

"What time is it now?"

"Early enough you ain't missed your fight yet, but you're gonna." Jaunty Hat didn't bother hiding his feral smile. "Boss Lady says we just babysit you until it's over, then you're free to be on your way. What say you be a good little prisoner and sit tight? Don't make us all miserable?"

Were it just my future on the docket for the fight, I might have taken up his offer. The tranquilizers still seeped through my system, and the grogginess hit me something vicious as the nausea receded. Even if I could get free, it wasn't the best state to be fighting in, not against unknowns like Hockney.

But it wasn't just my future I fought for, and his condescension pissed me off. I sucked in a slow breath and let it fill my lungs, bracing subtly as I could. Jaunty Hat smirked at me, confident the tape would hold, but I'd spent enough time around folks like the Captain to know a restraint's weaknesses. If you can't break the bonds, break the object they attach you to. I pushed my weight sideways, twisting instead of pushing, and the flimsy chair protested the sudden movement.

Jaunty Hat's eyes went wide as one arm snapped off, the tape securing mee already tearing loose, and I whipped the broken wood at his face to back him off. Adrenaline flooded my system, taking the edge off the pain and nausea, and I ripped my other arm free with a satisfied grin. Jaunty Hat produced a knife from a sheath beneath his jacket, a long blade designed for gutting men, not cutting steak. It sliced through the air, arching towards my stomach, and I brought my arm up in a clumsy block equal parts clinging tape and broke wood. Knives were always bad news. No fighter—no matter their experience—emerged from a knife fight without getting cut up along the way.

"Sit down, Princess," Jaunty Hat said, his knife held up in a crude guard. It wove back and forth, a serpent ready to strike, but there wasn't much skill behind it. "We get paid if you miss the fight. Doesn't matter if it's because you're cut up, or tranqued into a stupor."

I wasn't in the best fighting shape, not with my head still swimming from the drugs and the chair's remains still taped to my arms and legs, but I motioned for him to make his move. Jaunty Hat wet his lips and circled, trying to get an angle on me. I turned with him, ripping the chair's arm free, giving myself a solid chunk to use as a club. I held the make-shift weapon in a steady grip, eschewing useless movement. Jaunty Hat eyed me, gauging his chances, but the blade made him overconfident. He lunged, and I clubbed his elbow, followed it up with a sharp rap to the temple. The knife skittered from his grip and he went down on one knee, giving me an opening to put the wood against his neck and squeeze until he went limp.

I lowered his body to the floor and peeled off the tape and broken chair, kicking his knife beneath the shelves. Whatever the local statues against kidnapping and self-defense applied here, I didn't want the complications a stabbing engendered if SecDiv got involved.

Fingers punching the keypad alerted me to Jaunty Hat's buddy returning with my water, the eight soft beeps followed by an ominous click. I took a position by the doorway, pressed flat so he wouldn't see me first thing when he stepped inside. The door slid open and the second guy entered, a lurching behemoth who weighed over a hundred and eight kilos, his prodigious stomach leading the way. He wouldn't move fast in a fight, but didn't need to. I went low, smashing my make-shift club against his knee, bringing him to the ground. I followed it with a tooth-rattling shot to the head and scrambled through the open door before it resealed and trapped me inside.

They'd stored me in a back room just off the Lotus kitchens, but the droids and low-level wage saves working the heaters and stoves back there barely gave me a second glance. I found my comm and my jacket on a counter beside the storage room, securing both as I made a beeline for the rear door.

NINE

The fresh, salt-laden air washed over the unpleasant edge of tranquilizers still in my system. I drew deep breaths as I hustled down the narrow alley I found myself in, heading for the busy street to my right. With luck, I could disappear into the crowds before Mitch Jensen or her goons could try to reacquire me.

My plan lasted a hundred yards, which is when I realized my head wasn't clearing, sweat poured off me like I'd just run fifty clicks in cardio training, and the heaviness in my gut threatened to end in vomit if I continued to push the pace. My vision swam as the adrenaline faded and my gait reeled like a drunkard, and it took everything I had to fumble with the comm and put in a call to Zadie.

"Damn, you look like ass," she said.

"Drugged," I said. "Kidnapped. Trying to get back to the ship, but they're after me."

To her credit, Zadie skipped right past asking questions, stowing 'em for later. How and why I'd been tranqued and stashed was secondary to ensuring my location and safety. "Drop a pin. We're on our way," she said. "Keep the comm open long as you can."

"Roger."

I plowed my way down Fanton Avenue, careening through the tightly pressed crowd. Even in my lurching stupor I could sense the drones hovering overhead, mechanical eyes tracking my movement and reporting back to the local SecDiv. There were good odds Agent Fring would pick me up if Mitch Jensen's men didn't. The lesser evil, but still bad.

A fresh wave of nausea sent me stumbling into the railing surrounding a bathhouse's small gardens. I pinched my nose, trying to hold my stomach contents in, but my gorge rose and brought everything I'd eaten for the last eight hours with it. My stomach contents splattered over orderly petunia rows, and an irate employee emerged from the door screaming obscenities about drunken spacers and paying for the replacement blooms.

Someone fell in beside me, claimed my arm with a tight grip. "Nothing to worry about, love. Fresh from space, this one, and too much oxygen left her queasy." Jaunty Hat handed over a credit stick, his voice laced with smarmy charm. "This should take cover the damage, yeah? All good?"

A shadow fell across me, his buddy Lurch falling in on the other side. They hemmed me in, cutting off potential escape routes, and Lurch stretched an enormous arm across my shoulders to peel me away from the flowers. The irate garden owner flicked her eyes from me, to the thugs who'd showed up in my wake, to the credit stick in Jaunty Hat's hand. Both kidnappers bore bruises from my earlier assault. She swallowed and decided on discretion over valor.

"Yes, fine. More than takes care of it," she said. Jaunty Hat beamed at her as Lurch hustled me down the street, two bruised thugs escorting a drunken spacer through the pristine streets. I went along, all meek and mild, not bothering to struggle, because I knew one thing my kidnappers didn't.

By now, Zadie Jayne had a steady ping on my comm. My pursuers might trash the device, but my crew knew I'd found myself in trouble. In White Harbor, where SecDiv watches everything, it wouldn't take long for her to hack the feeds and track our route.

I grinned, despite my predicament. Lurch and Jaunty Hat were eleven kinds of fucked. I may be the *Viking Maiden*'s champ, but there's naught on Captain Rackham's crew who can't hold their own in a scuffle. Big Wade emerged from an alleyway and charged across the street. Jaunty caught the hammer of feet against cobbles and turned, but Wade slammed into him like an overprotective wrecking ball and knocked back three feet

Lurch didn't realize his partner was down until Jaunty hit the floor. The big fella let me go, spun on his heel to face the new threat. Lurch brought his hands up, ready to brawl, and Wade dropped his centre of gravity and shot in to grab Lurch around the waist.

I figure a guy like Lurch didn't get manhandled often. The smart call when someone's grabbed your waist is scooting your legs back and leaning your weight against them, making yourself harder to pick up. Lurch flailed with all four limbs, trying to knock Big Wade's arms free. Allowed Wade to grab hold of Lurch's leg and flip the big man with a suplex, driving his victim into the cobblestones headfirst with all Wade's strength behind the throw. Lurch's skull cracked against stone and echoed off the buildings. The big man went limp, sure-as-shit knocked-the-fuck-out and lucky to escape without breaking his neck.

Jaunty got his feet under him and brought his knife to bear on Wade. The loss of Lurch rattled him badly, but he figured he could gut Big Wade and get me back to my store-room prison. Wade's eyes tracked the knife and he backed off, feeding Jaunty's confidence.

Poor bastard never saw Zadie Jayne coming up behind him. She slipped in, smooth as a hot laser boring a hole through butter, and claimed Jaunty's wrist. It bent one way, forcing him to release the blade, then torqued another until Jaunty's joints strained and he unleashed a strangled hiss.

Jaunty attempted to twist free, but it didn't do him no good. For all he had a good extra foot on Zadie, he didn't have her training. Zadie broke two of his fingers, then dislocated his elbow for good measure. Jaunty ended up on his knees, weeping from the searing pain. Regarded it as a damn blessing when Zadie kneed him in the skull and knocked him to the floor.

Big Wade hauled me upright and held me steady. "Hell, Valk, you doing okay?"

"Better'n if you hadn' shown." My words slurred together, and Zadie Jayne checked me over before I'd got the last word out. She tested my pulse and thumbed my eyelids back, examining my pupils.

"Drugged," she said. "Someone's trying to tip the balance here before the fight even starts."

"Just drank some tea," I slurred. "Doing Stig a favor."

"Well, there's your mistake." Zadie shook her head. "We'll need to find someone to sub for her. Get on the horn with Cap."

"No!" I pulled myself upright, and for the first time in a minute, it didn't feel like I'd tip over again. "Ain't down, just a little groggy. No worse 'an fighting drunk!"

"Hardly the best argument for letting you square up," Zadie said.

"I c'n do it." I shrugged off Wade's grip and put my guard up, throwing a few test punches. "Got to do it for the Cap'n. Save the ship."

"We got to get off the street first," Wade said. "SecDiv will have eyes on the scuffle back there, and you know they're going to rain hell on us for public brawling before this gets straightened out."

"Agreed. Let's get her to the Captain. It's her these assholes are messing with, and she can make the call."

Big Wade looped my arm over his shoulder and nudged me into motion. "You think she'd mind if I tracked down Stig Jensen to wring his damn bull neck?"

"Kid, I think your aunt would be a little proud. Then she'd yell at you for picking a fight you ain't ready to win just yet."

Wade laughed, and I laughed right alongside him. My brain wasn't working straight just yet, and I still felt hellishly woozy. Lacking any connection to my own feelings, I accepted Wade's reaction as a cue and adopted merriment as the socially acceptable emotion du jour.

TEN

I emerged from a murky blackness for the second time in a day, only it rated as a far better wake up than the first. They'd stashed me in a small canvas tent with a drip attached to my arm. Big Wade huddled on the small bench beside me, pretending to be absorbed in the research on his terminal. I pushed myself upright, gritting my teeth against the lurching nausea, and Wade reached over to steady me. "Take it easy. We're still flushing tranquilizers from your system."

I brushed his hand away, focused on breathing steadily and letting the world settle into an equilibrium. Every inhalation brought the salt water and ozone scents of the harbor, helped me focus so the tent flaps dancing in the breeze didn't hurt like the thump of a hammer. Outside, the familiar hum of a fight crowd warming up for a bout, including familiar voices from the *Maiden*'s crew who'd gathered to watch me defend the ship's pride. Wade headed for the opening and alerted those nearby that I'd woken up, and both Zadie and Captain Rackham pushed their way inside.

Rackham took one look at me and swore a blue streak, hauling out the kind of language I'd only heard her use one time, when we got caught in an asteroid cloud. That time she'd been preoccupied by the damage our hull sustained and how much it'd cost to repair things if we got free. Her concern suggested she'd bet hard on this fight, and slotting a replacement in disrupted her plans.

"I'm going to find Stig Fucking Jensen and wring his damn fool neck," she said.

"How long we got?" I slurred.

"You called ninety minutes before the fight's scheduled to start," Zadie said. "Took us twenty minutes to track you down, another ten to get you here. We've been flushing your system for the last half-hour."

"So I'm due in the cage in thirty?"

"You ain't fighting," Captain Rackham said. "I ain't comfortable putting you out there, Valk—"

"Ain't about being comfortable!" I said. "Who else you got? We all scouted Hockney's fight footage, and we know what he can do. I figure I'm good to go once I hit the cage. He'll pop me in the mouth and get the adrenaline flowing, and from there I just keep punching until I've busted him up good and proper."

I shucked off my shirt and shoes, planning to make good on my promise, and it took Wade, Zadie, and the Captain combined to keep me from reeling out there in my skivvies.

"Forget this," Captain Rackham said. "I can't put you out there in good conscience, and we can't forfeit the fight. Who can we substitute?"

Big Wade wrapped me in a bear hug, holding me tight as I threatened to whip any replacement they might name. Zadie Jayne gave me a shot in the arm, some drug from her kit, and straightened my head enough to cease making their lives difficult. "Pickings are slim," she said. "Everyone expected Valkyrie to fight, so Deakin and McAllister are both drunk, and Lamont's off seeing her girl. The next choice would have been Stig, but he's no longer an option."

"It may have to be you," the Captain said, but Zadie waved him off.

"Hockney's too far out of my weight class, Cap, and he's good. Not saying I won't make the attempt, but if you're looking for the dubya here, I'm the underdog."

The Captain swore beneath her breath, and I fought through the fog enough to hatch myself a plan. "Wade might be the next choice, Cap. He's got the size, and his grappling game isn't bad. If he can keep Hockney from taking his back, he stands a fighting chance."

Big Wade coughed and spluttered in surprise, and Zadie arched an eyebrow. Captain Rackham stood her ground and stroked her chin, running a thumb from the scar below her right eye to the base of her ear. "Ain't the worst plan," she said. "Ain't the best. I'd rather not risk our future on it. No offense, kid."

"None taken," Wade said.

"We still need options, then."

Everyone's foreheads creased as we ran through the options, but my brain coughed up a different name. "Fring!"

"Don't recall hiring anybody with the name," Cap said.

"He's SecDiv," I said. "Gave me a warning not to brawl, on-planet. Old friend of my parents. He's had drones on me since I came ashore, knew my reputation."

"Not seeing how getting you arrested helps," Wade said, but Rackham and Zadie were already doing the math and seeing the possibilities.

"Technically, they'd be coming for Wade and me," Zadie said. "Valk was a victim, not a participant. He'll need statements. Maybe delay the fight an hour or two. Buy her time to sober up."

"Lance won't buy it," The Captain said. "Too much risk SecDiv will crash the party and rip apart both ship's crews with charges. They'll want to do this now, and Lance's cold enough to call for a forfeit just to claim the victory. We need Valkyrie's Agent friend to step in during the bout, I think. Declare things a draw, so everyone saves face."

I furrowed my brow, wondering why Fring's friendly warning and scrutiny hadn't extended to stepping in when I'd been chased by goons. "Might work. Agent Fring ignored the street brawl so far, Hockney and I breach local regulations hard the moment we square off. If he's like most Marines who worked with my mother, he's got the ambitions to rise up the ranks. Busting a fight like this looks good, so all I've gotta do is last the first round, maybe part of the second."

"That's *if* he's been watching the right drone footage," Zadie said.

I beamed at her. "I'm assuming somebody with your skills could ensure he sees what needs seeing."

"Maybe," Zadie said. "Local SecDiv is running pretty decent encryption. Might take me a minute to ease my way in without drawing too much attention."

"I'm not the biggest fan," Rackham said. "Too many variables we can't control."

"Way I'm thinking, I count as the least-worst option."

Captain Rackham scowled, but she knew I'd assessed her choices and come to the right answer. "Get started. I'll see if I can buy us some time."

She swung around, leaning her weight against the crutch, and left the tent to go argue with the *Bester*'s captain. Zadie exchanged a long glance with Big Wade, the terminal already in her hands. "Get her ready, and leave the drip on long as you can," she instructed. "This is going to take some concentration."

"Roger that," Wade said.

In an authorized fight, the pageantry and ritual give you some breathing space. An hour or two in the locker room with your team, clearing your head before the fight. The announcements and entry music, where you can size one-another up and try to get into a fella's head before throwing the first punch. For a big fight, organized months in advance, there might even be some jawing for the streams before the bout arrives. I know fighters who love the folderol, and those who come into each bout with a purity of purpose. Zadie Jayne thrives on it, although she's a fair hand in a street scrap as well.

Pageantry's never been my scene. Me, I want to go out there and throw leather as quick as possible, give the adrenaline an outlet. Holding fast while Big Wade stripped me down and taped up my fists proved a short-course in agony, although my pulse still quickened at the thought of stepping into the cage and putting my fists up.

Wade gave me a wary look. "You sure, boss?"

I wasn't, but I flashed him a confident grin. "Relax, kid. I've fought in worse conditions than this," I said. "Hell, once upon a time I beat four Moscow King crew members while blind drunk and struggling to stand."

Big Wade didn't look convinced. "Still a hell of a gigantic risk you're taking in this one."

"Think of this way: there's a young woman out there willing to drug me in order to make sure the *Maiden* comes out second best in this one. You think I'm going to give her the satisfaction?"

This time, he smiled. "Naw, boss. Not you," he said.

Across the tent, Zadie looked up from her terminal and flashed us a thumbs up.

"One round," I said. "I can last one round. Let's get this party started, yeah?"

Wade said nothing, but he removed the IV, and for the first time since downing a drugged cuppa tea, I stood without keeling sideways four steps later.

ELEVEN

The *Bester* was an old B-Class heavy hauler, rated for 23,000 containers and still using the old naval design to allow her to berth in water ports. A sleek old girl, compared to the newer models, which are nothing more than flying blocks built and destined to live their lives floating through the black, never expecting to touch down planet-side nor host a gathering on their open decks. They'd berthed her in the outer docks, far from the wall where they do the heavy unloading, and the *Bester*'s crew formed a howling mob outnumbering the *Maiden*'s by two-to-one. They'd contracted a makeshift on the forecastle, with enough space for a crowd to gather. The bodies clustered around the port-side guns told me where Hockney warmed up, egged on by cheering crewmates. The starboard side belonged to the *Viking Maiden*'s crew, determined not to let their smaller number equate to a less vocal support. Ships are territorial and have been since the age of sail. A by-product of the isolation and relying on your fellows to keep everything afloat.

Captain Rackham lurked by the cage, exchanging words with her friend Beatrice Lance and a stern woman I recognized as the *Star Eagle's* Captain, Cassie Majors. Whatever else had gone wrong, we'd secured an honest referee. Good news for my plan to last through the first round.

I pounded my fists together and loosened my neck as Wade

slipped my mouth guard in. The *Bester*'s deck proved cold against my bare feet, which gave me something to focus on beyond my heavy arms and churning stomach. Wade clapped me on the back, and Zadie emerged with her kit in hand. We made our way towards the cage, threading through the *Maiden*'s crew gathered on the starboard side. Familiar faces reached out to bump fists or shout encouraging words, egging me on.

I did my best to ignore them all, just as I set aside how my body felt, even Zadie and Wade's presence. Everything narrowed to the opposite corner, where Addison Hockney strode to the makeshift cage. He moved languorously, loose-limbed and confident, his dark eyes gleaning in the band between his thick thatch of dark beard and tight-clipped hair.

Captain Rackham joined us by the cage and whispered a few words in my ear. I barely heard them above the raucous crowd, all bellowed shouts and stomping feet. Hockney climbed into the cage first, raising his hands to the *Bester*'s crew. They responded with a roar mighty enough to alert every SecDiv agent in ten miles a shady donnybrook was in the offering.

Zadie placed her forehead against mine, one hand against the back of my skull. "You've got to be feeling like ass about now."

She wasn't wrong. Beneath the adrenaline, I could still sense the price I paid to be there: a sharp headache in my sinuses, my head all fuzzy and packed in foam. But my adrenaline ran hot now, and my body knew what to do in a fight better than my brain ever could. I clapped her shoulder and assured her I'd be just fine out there, once the bell rang, and she took me at my word.

Cassie Majors from the Star Eagle didn't waste any time with pageantry, bringing me and Hockney to the middle long enough to inform us of the rules, then calling for the handshake. We thumped fists and backed away, already in the zone.

Outside the cage, two pots clanked together as a makeshift bell, and then me and Hockney were at it. He came at me in a port-side stance, leading with his left. A rapid-fire feint to get me covered up, so he could shoot in for the take-down and get this wrapped up fast. Pity for him I'd seen this part, at least, in the scant footage Zadie uncovered. I'd done my time against southpaws and it didn't throw me off. I met his shoot with a wide sprawl, my balance spread to keep us both upright, and walloped his skull with elbows to discourage his efforts before they bore fruit.

There are damn few folks with a head hard enough to take a half-dozen elbows to their temple, and Hockney wasn't among their number. He backed off, and I went after him, throwing punches and kicks to keep him honest and focused on escape.

Hockney retreated into the cage and waited, grinning behind his guard. He motioned with his fingers, inviting me to stick with my approach, and the belligerent, dope-stupid part of my brain wanted to obey. Wade in and hammer him with power rights until he fell against the floor.

But the other half of my head, running on adrenaline and instinct, recognized the trap.

Problem is, my woozy ass didn't care, and I went at Hockney like a bulldozer in the first round, not even bothering to get an angle in my eagerness to stand and bang. Stupid way to a fight—you'd expect it from a green rookie with no ground-game, placing their trust in the puncher's chance—but Hockney didn't seize on the advantage I'd handed to him. He bottled up and let me welter him, giving ground all the while.

Way I figure he'd done his homework for this, studied my usual approach. Figured I'd come in slow and wily, feel out his defenses in the first exchange. Coming in crude and messy struck him as a trick, and he gave ground when he could have taken control and choked my stoned ass out.

Reckless anger and cognitive dissonance carried me through the opening minutes, but it cost me bad once Hockney realized I had no wheel within my wheel. He took me down in the third minute, and Hockney was murder on the floor. Strong and fast, with a focused assault to get past my guard and take my back, looking to set up the rear naked choke and ensure the TKO. Adrenaline surged once I hit the canvas, chasing off the worst of the fog. I wrapped my legs around Hockney's torso and fought to control his arms.

I had seen Zadie Jayne fight and she excelled at fighting underneath, turning defense into a winning hold capable of ensuring her opponent tapped out. My jiu jitsu isn't as strong as hers, but I'd trained with her enough to recognize what came next. Hockney and I tussled on the mat for the last ninety seconds, and he rained bombs down on my head when it became clear he couldn't flip me over. Caught me good with a left-handed punch, splitting the skin above my right eye and splattering the deck with blood. If he'd landed it two seconds earlier, the match belonged to him. Instead, the bell rang, giving me a chance to retreat to the corner and get the wound patched up before it impaired my vision.

I retreated to my corner, where Zadie and Big Wade sprang into action. Wade gave me water and washed down my face, while Zadie tended to my cuts, sponging my eyebrow and applying adrenaline to close the wound and stop the bleeding. "What the fuck you doing?" she said. "You're fighting like a maniac."

"Almost worked," I fired back.

"Luck," Zadie said. "Not skill." She wiped gel over my injury, slicking it closed as best she could.

"You get a line?"

"Yeah. I've been monitoring their comms."

"Any sign SecDiv's showing up to arrest our ass?"

Zadie didn't say a damn thing, and even fight-addled and high on adrenaline, I knew our gambit wouldn't play out. SecDiv wasn't coming to arrest anyone, which meant this fight lasted until Hockney or I knocked the other out.

TWELVE

Zadie finished tending my wounds, and the Captain took her spot, weathered face pressed so close to mine I could feel hot breath against my skull. "He's rattled," she said. "Hockney thinks he knows you, because he's studied. He thinks he can predict how you're going to play it. Buy yourself some time this round. Make him work for it."

My nostrils flared as I took Cap's words in, feigning confidence in her advice. Zadie swapped in for the old woman, squirting fresh water into my mouth. "You sure you should be out there, Valk? Captain will have my ass if you get hurt here."

I wanted to reassure her, promise the old fight-or-flight instinct had cleared the cobwebs now he'd popped me in the face. I wanted to tap into the old Valkyrie bravado and declare I had this in the bag.

But Hockney had rattled me. He was fast, and he was powerful, and he'd have been a tough fight if I'd come into this one hundred per cent and prepared to throw down. Here and now, drug-woozy and hurting, I recognized the real trouble I'd got myself into and how much the Captain could. The thought burnt through me, blades of shame and anger waging a battle over which sucked more. I focused my stare on Hockney, perched in his corner. I breathed slow and steady, steeling my focus. SecDiv wasn't coming. Nothing mattered but taking the bastard out any way I could. Which meant I needed to play it smarter, use the lessons from every beating I'd taken and every fight where I'd been outclassed.

Hockney smirked at me, showing off the black mouth guard. He raised both eyebrows and tilted his chin. A silent challenge to come back for more, and the cockiness pissed me off so bad I looked forward to the second round.

Hockney came in targeting my eyebrow wound, looking for the ref stoppage if he could bust me open and obscure my vision with flowing blood. He put in a decent effort for a fighter who hates the striking game, but his heart wasn't in it—too late I realized he'd targeted my injury to force a defense, leaving him openings to exploit. The plan's simplicity and effectiveness put a swagger in his step, but I came into the second with a clearer head and less churn in my roiling stomach. When he came after my eyebrow, I saw an opening and caught him good with a short right hand to the floating rib. The stiff punch delivered an opening for a powerhouse left to Hockney's eye.

It rocked him, a little reminder Dana Valkyrie wasn't going down easy for anyone, and by the round's end his ribs were bruise-dark, his face puffed up from blunt force trauma. The *Viking Maiden*'s crew raised a hullaballoo when they saw me firing back, more like the Valkyrie they knew than the wild-woman who'd fought the first. I rode their cheers as I pressed the advantage on Hockney, whittling him down with a stick-and-move assault. He abandoned anything fancy and went back to his bread and butter, shooting in for takedowns where his ground-game had the advantage, and it took everything I had to sprawl and avoid grappling him on the mat.

We hit the bell, running more-or-less even, both battered and hurting from the struggle. Zadie Jayne went to work on my cuts and bruises, and across the ring Hockney's cutman worried at the rapidly puffing black eye he'd earned with his hubris. It was my turn to smile across the ring and swagger into the third. What's good for the gander is good for the goose, after all, and I'd earned my points instead of getting lucky.

The tenor of a fight changes in the third. It's your last, in some fights. Halfway in others. In either case, ten straight minutes beating an opponent down is harder than most non-fighters think, and adrenaline's less effective after running hard for so long. Used to be I'd get right reckless in the third, impatient to end things at all costs, but years spent traveling with Captain Rackham and listening to her advice taught me the merits of caution and a measured approach.

Hockney came in fatigued, leaving holes in his defense so wide they could only be a trap. I used my jab to keep him at range, content to be a small target. If he wanted to get the tap-out, I'd make him work for it. Expend the energy and burn through his reserves, even if meant burning through my own diminishing tank. In a pinch, I can wear a fella down over a five-round fight without breaking a sweat, and I prayed he'd seen enough footage to see my standard slow-grind strategy play out. If he assumed I had energy, rather than the fatigue and pain weighing me down, I could hold him off a little a little longer.

Exhaustion meant the fight became a mental game. Hockney broke first, shooting in for the take-down, and I sprawled my weight to block it. Most wrestlers change tack when they can't get you down, rather than leave their head open to elbows, but Hockney's centre of gravity was low, and the gods built the fucker like a warhorse. He powered me back until my spine hit the cage.

I grabbed at his skull, trying to clinch up and hold with all I had. Hockney fought for a one-handed overhook, his left hand trying to lay claim to my wrist. He ground his forehead against my jaw, used his leg to pin mine down and prevent me from firing off hard knees into his midsections. Pinning me against the cage bought him time and control, and the scorecard would go his way for the round if neither of us secured the knock-out. Worse, if he could get me down, I had no defense against the ground and pound. Short jabs hammered into my ribs from below, softened me up for something worse.

I stomped my heel against Hockney's foot in desperation, felt toes break beneath the impact. It bought me a few much-needed seconds, enough to shove him back. Hockney steadied, his right hand already looping in, but I plugged him, my left hook sailing in over his strike. It rocked him hard, but he still didn't want to go down. He brought his hands up to protect his skull, and this time I fell for the set-up. I came in feeling confident, ready to drop Hockney where he stood, when he suckered me. Ducked under my arm and grabbed a leg, toppled me to the mat.

There's an elegance to some fights, when you are both on your feet and swinging wildly, but finesse goes away the moment you're grappling on the floor. What started as sweet science soon resembles a scrap between children, with Hockney trying to flip me over while I kicked free with my other heel. My game plan to burn through his reserves had failed, and I sucked air harder than I should have. The drugs still taxed my system, on top of the beating I'd taken, and I wasn't as close to one hundred percent as experience told me I should be.

I counted it as a small mercy when the bell rung while we tussled, saving me from the inevitable moment when Hockney locked in his hold and tore me up. As it was, I staggered back to my corner and clamped my teeth shut. The bodywork he'd done meant I needed to puke, but it would award Hockney the TKO by default. My gorge rose and I fought it, swallowing it down, even as the acid burned my throat and The Captain came in with water to rinse the taste out.

"Two rounds," Rackham said. "Last two more and you can draw with this asshole, and we walk out with our heads held high."

I didn't think I had two more in me, but I didn't say nothing out loud.

"I'm counting on you, Valkyrie," the Captain said. "You're the hardest woman I know."

It hurt to breathe. It hurt to swallow. It hurt to fucking move.

But I knew things were just as bad for Hockney, and I looked forward to the coming round.

THIRTEEN

Half the fight game is mental, and I needed every edge I could grab. That meant getting to my feet long before the bell, focused on the far side of the ring where they tended to Hockney's cuts and bruises. I'd given Mitch Rhoden the entire speech about why I wouldn't throw a fight, not with all the *Maiden*'s crew counting on me alongside the Captain's wager, but I didn't need to give it here. The Captain knew I wasn't backing down by the set of my shoulders and the hard line of my jaw, and she knew why the moment the *Maiden*'s crew hollered and cheered me on as I stretched, showing no fear of what might come. I locked eyes with Hockney and glared through the last seconds, putting everything I had into the illusion I was a relentless monster determined to rip him apart."

Captain Rackham smiled despite herself. "Good," she said. "I worried there he'd beaten the fight out of ya, what with everything else going on. Don't mess around this time—you see the angle, so go in for the kill. You fought his fight in the last round. This time, it's all your way."

I rolled my shoulders, then my neck. Zadie's attempts to flush my system meant I didn't want to keep over at the movement, but my limbs didn't move right yet. They felt weightless, like the one-two shots of gravity and fatigue weren't doing their job. Troubling, but I'd fought through worse in the cage when my bell got rung by an opponent's strike. The trick lay in presenting an impassive face, unaffected by your wounds. The *Maiden's* crew screaming blue murder as Hockney's team finished ministering to his wounds. Beatrice Lance abandoned the ringside crew first, disappearing into the howling, faceless throng comprised by the *Bester* crew. Lance didn't matter—she was the Captain's fight. My job revolved around knocking Hockney out, and I intended to do so early in the round.

The bell rang to kick off the fourth, and I came at Hockney sideways, circling around the makeshift cage instead of going straight at him with all I had. The *Bester's* crew hollered and jeered, figuring I feared their fighter, but kept my focus on Hockney's dark eye and the hitch in his step from the broken toe. The poor bastard sucked down deep breaths, prepaying for a furious assault I declined to bring against him. He stumbled, and I gave him a moment to catch his wind, feel the fatigue setting in. I let him breathe and focused on the angles, looking to come in on the blind side where his eye was closing up. By the fourth, a fight's a game of attrition. Who's got the wind, who's still got tricks left in the tank and who's got injuries to be exploited? Switch up your game plan and a fighter gets nervous, wondering what you're going to pull and what he missed when scouting ya. Hockney sucked wind because he feared he wouldn't get the chance once I came at him and pushed the pace.

I tightened up and closed the distance between us, trying to get an angle. He put his guard high, expecting me to lead with my fists, and I swung a low kick at his knee to keep the bastard honest. Hockney danced back, giving ground to lure me in, and I settled just outside his reach and kept the pressure on, waiting for him to make the first move.

He broke after a minute, feinting left like he wanted to fire off a strike, weaving right to go after my arm and leverage me to the floor. Too clumsy by half to sucker me in, but he was tired, and he was sweating what I had up my sleeve. I shot in past his hands and grabbed Hockney around the middle. He fired off desperate elbows, trying to get me to let go, but I accepted the pain and focused all I had on tossing his hundred and twenty kilos with a belly-to-belly suplex.

The move caught Hockney by surprise, and his limbs windmilled as I tossed him. Land it right, and a suplex can end a fight fast—it takes a tough bastard to get back on his feet after going into the floor head first—but Hockney twisted to catch the worst on his shoulder. It still blasted all the air from his lungs, and when he winced as he raised his guard once more, I knew I'd hurt him good. His arm hung low and didn't move easily, and he couldn't hide the pain involved in holding it at the ready.

Now I pressed the advantage. I hammered Hockney across the ring, but he rallied and caught me with a right hook, which splayed my nose against my cheek. I rocked back on my heels, blood fountained from both nostrils, and he figured he'd caught me hard enough to play things his way for a stretch. The bastard shot in low, looking for take-down, but I caught him in a tight cinch and rattled him with a series of knees. He sagged and staggered, trying to wrench free, but only pushed me into the cage and pinned me there with his weight. For a moment, we fought deadlocked, strength against strength.

Then Hockney slipped free, reeling back on his heels, his guard not quite high enough. I swung in with a left hook to the jaw, throwing it hot and heavy as a meteor falling through atmosphere. He stumbled back and his knees went out, but he steadied himself and came back with a left-handed shot just as I followed through with my right. I tagged him good, but he hammered me in the chin damn near simultaneously, and we both went down hard.

I hit the ground back-first, my ears ringing from the impact, but instinct sent me clambering to my feet soon as I had my bearings. It wasn't pretty—Hockney's right had knocked me loopier than being drugged, and I veered left with a half-hearted guard up, not entirely altogether. Raw panic kept me moving, the utter certainty Hockney would pass my guard and tap me out in my current state, or get the TKO if I didn't have a defense at the ready.

I crashed into the cage and rolled against it, clutching at the chain links to hold myself upright. Bright lights sparked along the corner of my vision, and for a moment I feared he'd caught me, sent me crashing to the canvas in a KO handing victory over to the *Bester*. I felt half-out and defenseless as a kitten, but the bright flashes existed in the real world, not caused by the pounding my head had taken over the last twenty minutes. Too late, I smelt the teargas and caught the cries of surprise.

My groggy brain put it all together. A raid, finally, too little too late. SecDiv agents swarming over the *Bester*'s deck, calling warnings for everyone to stay put and keep their hands exposed.

I cast about, trying to reorient myself, and glimpsed Big Wade protecting the Captain. Beyond them, Zadie Jayne squared off against an armored, club-wielding agent. Across the cage, damn near slumbering where I'd dropped him, Addison Hockney struggled to shake off the knockout punch I'd delivered.

My heart surged even as the SecDiv agents warmed the cage, pistols drawn and covering everyone who'd been within their confines. Agent Fring pulled his cap off and glared at me, shaking his head in disappointment.

"Dana Valkyrie, I'm placing you under arrest."

I didn't have the energy to fight him.

FOURTEEN

SecDiv secured both crews at the local Security Centre, separating us out into different rooms to prevent a brawl breaking out. I found myself laid out on the steel bench. Cap and Wade kept the crew back while Zadie tended to my wounds. Consensus said I'd beaten Hockney, even though Major couldn't call the win before SecDiv swarmed the *Bester*.

Agents dropped by our cell every fifteen minutes, peeling away crew members to take a statement. I stayed put and licked my wounds, letting the fight pains settle over me. Nothing matches the post-fight exhaustion after the adrenaline leaves you, and I got a real feel for the trauma my body suffered at Hockney's massive fists. Few crew members returned to the cell after questioning, so our numbers whittled down until the barest handful. They called Wade, then Zadie Jayne, leaving me and Captain Rackham as the sole folks who hadn't been questioned yet.

Agent Fring and his compatriots stepped up to the cell's Plexiglas wall and called my name, which left the Captain to fly solo. We traded a look, and she gave me a curt nod, sending me off to answer the authorities' questions and leaving her without back up. It felt ten kinds of wrong, but I'd learned the hard way not to cross your average SecDiv agent when they're throwing their weight around. I stepped up, hurting and breathing shallow, and offered my hands for the cuffs.

Fring waved me off. "I'm thinking you're hurting bad enough without some extra weight to carry around."

He wasn't wrong, but I didn't want to show it. I followed them off to one of the interview rooms, a cramped space with so many sensors in the air they read your honesty in pupil twitches and unsteady voice modulations. Fring pointed me to a hard, plain chair and sat opposite me. He activated the recording and logged his name and the case details before turning his smile on me.

"I warned you not twenty-four hours ago, Ms Valkyrie. Unlicensed fights are illegal on Boros."

"And you don't offer a license for anything official," I said.

"Citizens are partial to a peaceful planet," Fring said. "Fighters get rowdy."

I flashed him a rueful smile and raised both palms as best I could with my hands cuffed together. "Ain't like I planned it. Just been an eventful twenty-four hours," I said.

"So I gather from your compatriots' statements. By all accounts, your captain pushed for a planet side. Multiple crew members claim tried to de-escalate before it turned into a reason for an all-out brawl."

He said it all reasonable, like he just wanted confirmation, but I recognized the trouble lurking in those words. The only thing more dangerous than a SecDiv agent gunning for you is a SecDiv agent pretending they might be on your side.

"Your crewmates offered some interesting details regarding tonight's fracas," Fring continued, leaning across the table and fixing me with an earnest look. "They also left some important gaps. I'm wondering if you can fill those spaces for me?"

"I'm here to cooperate," I said.

"Excellent. So, tell me, Ms. Valkyrie, did Aurelia Rackham pressure you to take this fight?"

I laughed at the suggestion. Couldn't help myself. Confusion flashed past Fring's stern features, and he drew back as if I'd stung him. "Did I say something funny?"

"Just yesterday, we reminisced about my unsuitability to

work alongside authority figures," I said. "You think Aurelia Rackham can pressure me into fighting a bout I didn't want?"

"She's a formidable woman, your captain..."

"Folks have suggested I'm a strong-headed ass myself," I said.

"Then you weren't coerced, or ordered to take part? She didn't hold your position over your head, promising to make your life miserable if you failed to comply."

"Ain't the Captain's way," I said. "I fought Hockney because I fight people, Agent. He offered an opportunity to test myself, and I wanted to find out if I could take him."

"You seemed determined to stay trouble free when we talked."

"At the time I hadn't met Hockney. He rubbed me wrong," I said.

"You realize, if you take the blame for this, we'll be holding you on Boros for thirty days until we can arrange a hearing. Your ship will depart and you'll lose your berth. It'll be harder to find a new berth, with a Borosian charge laid against your record. Any ship who signs you will be subject to greater scrutiny when they return, and on any planet you visit in network range. We work on a strict two-strikes-and-you're-out system here."

"Doesn't seem so bad," I said. "You've been okay company between the threats."

"This isn't a joke, Valkyrie."

"Agreed. It's a pain in the ass," I said.

"We don't want *you*." Fring glared at me across the table, fingers bunched into fists. "I know you were goaded into this by the Captain, pushed into fighting by a superior. I can sell that line and get you out of this, all you've gotta do is tell me Rackham pushed you into the fight. Gave you an order, or made you fear for your job if you said no the woman. Give me something and I can save you."

He went silent, outwardly stern, but his eyes pleaded with me to roll on the Captain and deliver the answer he wanted.

"I'm a grown woman, Fring. I make my own choices, and cop the fallout."

I met Fring's stare, refusing to back down, and he exhaled and sank back in his chair. The veteran ran narrow fingers over his clipped hair, finger. "You know, your blood tests show they drugged you in the last twenty-four hours. Perhaps you weren't in your right mind to make such decisions."

"I doubt that."

"You want to tell me what you've been taking, Valkyrie?"

"I don't know," I said. "A local teashop owner named Rhoden slipped me a micky while we drank a cuppa. Her cousin recently left our employ on the *Viking Maiden*."

"They tranquilized you?"

"Seems like."

"And you still fought?"

I fixed Fring with a wolfish grin. "I like to test myself. Captain wasn't pleased I stepped into the ring incapacitated, but I've never been one for listening to the authority figures around me."

Fring exhaled, venting irritation. He looked right at me. "I don't think you understand the scale here, how much shit you're really in. In the last twenty-four hours I've had complaints you disrupted a bathhouse, picked a fight at a local tea shop, vomited in a private garden, and engaged in a public brawl. Right now, my superiors are putting pressure on me to hang someone out to dry for this. I'd rather it wasn't you, because I respect your mother and family."

"My family name's Valkyrie."

"An affected nom de plume."

"Legally changed, not long after I left home. Only family I have these days, given my mother's disappointment in the choices I've made in life."

"Miss Valkyrie—"

"Agent Fring, you don't owe me any favors. I'm not throwing my captain out an airlock. I fought knowing the consequences, and I'm ready to face them."

Fring looked back at me. "I can't change your mind?"

I shook my head.

"Fine, let's start at the beginning," he said. "Tell me what occurred at the Bath House yesterday morning, and this time skip nothing."

I held his stare and cleared my throat, arranging everything in order before I began. Worst-case scenario, they'd arrest me and hold me for thirty days. Worst-case scenario, the *Maiden* would keep flying, doing the four-month trip to the next planet. I'd either find a new vessel or spend two years waiting for the Maiden to get a job ferrying to White Harbor again.

Or I'd message my family looking for aid, validating every assumption they had when I chose not to join the military.

Worst-case scenario, the *Maiden* left on time and the crew kept working. It would hurt letting them leave without me, but grounding one person made more sense than the whole damn ship.

FIFTEEN

They moved me from general holding to an overnight cell, three concrete walls with a fourth consisting of a single glass panel hard enough to survive a meteor impact. Each clear wall had a single maglocked door tucked into the corner, the sole exit once you'd been stuffed inside. Each cell contained two bunks embedded into the wall, one either side of a communal bathroom if I needed to relieve myself. I crawled across my cell and racked out, content to let my body recover from the beating I'd taken in the cage. Nothing I could do until morning anyway, and it wasn't like Agent Fring and his comrades hurried in to update me on the case.

I woke the next morning feeling stiff and sore, riding the emotional roller-coaster fighters encounter after a big bout. My stomach growled, eager to replace the calories I'd lost during the bout, and I couldn't remember eating anything after SecDiv brought us in.

On the *Maiden*, I'd start the day eating a large breakfast and downing a coffee. A light workout, stretching and a little cardio so I didn't calcify, then an afternoon spent talking things through with the Captain and enjoying a beer or two. In my ten-by-ten cell, I settled for doing push-ups and a slow pace from end-to-end. A SecDiv agent stopped by to deliver a hot, mushy sustenance. It might have been oatmeal at one point, might have been a fungal stew. I ate mechanically, feeling my jaw click with the effort. Settled in to replay events in my head and figure out what I could learn. A little trick I'd learned from the Captain, who believed all mistakes worth making, so long as you didn't make 'em twice.

As lunch approached, and my stomach rumbled once more, self-pity clawed at me and I imagined the *Viking Maiden*'s crew returning to the vessel. Checking in and preparing to get back to work, ready to load up and launch for another run through the Black, hauling the cargo the Captain sourced to the Macquarie Sector.

I wasn't sure what I'd do when my sentence concluded, or what ship might choose to hire a former chief engineer looking for a new gig. Odds were, I'd end up working underneath someone again. Working my way back up to chief engineer over time, the same way I'd earn myself the title of champ.

It held less appeal, compared to working the *Maiden*, but that ship had sailed—literally.

Agent Fring interrupted my melancholy at twelve-hundred hours, stepping in just before the lunch delivery. He took a position beside my cell, face pinched and angry as a Venusian storm stripping the armored hull off a warship. I pushed myself off the bunk and beamed at him, feigning a cheerfulness I couldn't feel. "Agent, a pleasure to see you again."

"Who did you call?" Fring spat the words, his irritation clear.

"Call?"

"All your flimflam about hating your mother, but it had to be someone in your family. Who else would have the stroke to make all this go away?"

"I'm not sure what you're talking about, Agent Fring."

He glared at me and punched the maglock code; the doors unsealing with a heavy clunk. "You're free to go," he said. "We've dropped all charges against you."

"Dropped?" My heart leapt at the word. I took a step towards the door, still expecting him to draw a club and launch an attack if I tried to leave.

"Message came down from the governing council ten minutes ago. All spacers involved in yesterday's brawl are to be released."

Fring squared his shoulders and looked straight ahead. "I'm here to escort you and process your release, Miss Valkyrie."

He escorted me through the SecDiv offices and returned my belongings, scant as they were given my fighting garb when they arrested me. Fring's face could have fouled an entire airlock, but he kept his tone civil and delivered me to the front door, where Big Wade and Zadie waited for me.

Zadie caught my worried glance, searching for the Captain. "Released three hours ago," she said. "SecDiv went hard, pinned everything on her. It seems the *Bester*'s captain is doing her best to ensure the charges stick. Rackham called in some old favors to make it go away."

"She couldn't have pulled those favors last night? Got us all sleeping in our own bunks?"

"Captain's a tricky woman. Wasn't willing to pull out the big guns until necessary. She tumbled Lance tried to pin all this on her, and pulling a fast one on us to get our next contract." Zadie opened her satchel and dug up a protein bar as she spoke, handing it over to salve my rumbling stomach. "Every spacer on the *Bester* claims the fight wasn't over when the raid started, and they're all claiming the bet is void until we can organize a rematch."

I chowed down on the bar she'd brought me and cogitated over her news. "I had him beat," I said.

"You did."

"Kinda pissed he'd dragged his feet," I said. "Or didn't drag his feet a little longer. Wanted the bastard to stop the fight, not mess up my victory."

Zadie and Wade traded a look. "Well," Zadie said, "that's where this gets interesting. Seems I wasn't the only anonymous tip called into Agent Fring yesterday. Captain had me tap the Bester's comms, just in case someone tried to broadcast the fight, and one of their crew sent out a message about the fight right after mine. Thirty seconds after they pinged Fring's comm, SecDiv swarmed over the deck."

I paused mid-chew, my eyebrows shooting up.

"Yeah," Zadie said. "Struck me as hinky too."

I swallowed and wiped a sleeve across my mouth. "You

figure they had the same plan as us? Call SecDiv if to stop the bout?"

"Naw." Big Wade's wide smile barely contained his chortle. "Auntie Rackham thinks it's bigger than that. See, Zadie dug up some service records."

My eyes switched back to the Maiden's first mate, and she held up four fingers as a visual aid. "Agent Fring—" she wiggled her pinkie finger "—decorated marine come SecDiv agent investigating organized crime in White Harbor. Regularly worked with Lance's intelligence unit before she became a private citizen. Can't break the security on the records of their opps together, but they're old buddies from way back."

Zadie folded down her pinkie and ring finger, and my stomach rumbled. Wade fetched me another protein bar as Zadie continued her explanation.

"This is where Cap and I pulled together a theory," she said. "Lance and the *Bester* racked up a few bad runs. They've got debts, and it costs a lot to keep a ship that size running and adequately crewed. They need a good cargo, and they need operational credits, and they figure two birds, one stone. Pick a freighter with a high value haul, cripple their crew and sweep in to save the client left in the lurch when the original ship can't deliver as promised. They charge a premium for the job, and do a decent side-hustle on bets around the fight."

"Wild theory," I said. "Lots of conjecture."

"You'd think. Except Fring's history shows four major busts in the last eight years. All of them breaking up fights, all of them followed by a mass arrest that kept a ship in port for months. Dock records show the *Bester* departing not long after those bouts conclude. Word on the street is the Bester's champ won every one of those fights, too, yet they somehow escaped prosecution."

If I hadn't been chewing, my teeth would have ground to nubs at the news. "Well, that ain't sporting," I said.

Big Wade clapped a huge mitt against my spine. "You're the one always tellin' me fightin's an ugly business, Valk."

"True enough," I said. "Is the Captain pissed?"

"Angrier than a cat caught in an airlock when the seals pop," Zadie said. "Seems Lance's been ten kinds of scarce since the fight, although our client got a message she'd be taking over the *Maiden*'s run since our crew was indisposed. Rackham sorted it out and we're setting off on-schedule, but Cap's been piecing things together since then, figuring out the hustle. Still hasn't got everything down yet."

"What's left?"

Zadie wiggled the other two fingers. "Stig Rhoden and his cousin," she said. "Captain's not buying they drugged you on the off chance you'd win."

"Should have," Wade said. "Given she did."

"Ain't over until the referee calls it."

"True," Zadie said. "But we figured we'd stop by the tea house, ask Stig's cousin a few pressing questions. Want to come along?"

I wolfed down the protein bar's last mouthfuls, taking the edge off my raging hunger. "Now you mention it, I'm still a little peckish. Think I'd try one of their sandwiches."

"Can't be worse than their tea," Wade said.

SIXTEEN

We headed for the Lotus, and I showed Zadie and Wade the back way in, slipping through the alley and the door to the kitchens, where harried chefs and porters focused on serving fragrant meals and fresh pots of tea. The kitchen staff eyed us as we entered, wary, but between my fresh bruises and Wade's vast bulk, they decided against tangling with us. We nodded our hellos and took the back way up, heading up the stairs towards Mitch Rhoden's office.

Halfway up, I caught Mitch's voice, and I motioned for Zadie and Wade to slow themselves down and use a little stealth. We stole up close, and I pressed an ear to the door, and I heard the fast-paced conversation on the far side. I recognized the voices in play: Mitch and her cousin, Stig; Jaunty Hat and his sidekick, Lurch; and, last of all, staying calm and cold as ice, Captain Lance of the *Bester*.

"You were supposed to soften her up," Lance said, her voice laced with controlled anger. "You said, 'leave it to me, Bea,' and I made the assumption you could deliver."

"Don't pawn this on me," Mitch Rhoden said in a voice harder and meaner than I thought any tea merchant could ever lay on. "Fring was supposed to push her buttons. Stig was meant to ear her out, get her all good and riled. I drugged the woman and locked her down, pumped her full of enough tranquilizers into her system to take her out for a star's damned week."

"I warned you all not to underestimate her." Stig Rhoden's voice, surly and laced with a subtle I-told-you-so he dared not say out loud. "Valkyrie's been the *Maiden*'s champ four years now, and Rackham takes pride in hiring the best damn fighters to be on her crew, and she makes 'em better."

"You said you could beat her," Mitch snarled.

"I said I had a good chance. Nothing's certain, which is why we had back-ups. Sent her here..."

"Enough." Jaunty Hat's harsh, rasping voice cut through Stig's excuses. "We're not here to debrief on what went wrong. We did our part, and we want our money."

"Money!" Mitch Rhoden's voice, full of contempt and scorn. "You couldn't even keep the woman back here half-dead and tied to a chair."

"We did the job, and we get paid," Jaunty Hat said. "I'd hate for our professional relationship to sour over an incident like this. I believe—"

A hard slap cut off Jaunty Hat's rhetoric, and for a moment the room fell silent. Then everyone scrambled, Lurch roaring and throwing hard punches. Mitch Rhoden squeaked, and a gunshot broke the silence.

We decided we'd heard enough. Big Wade hit the door with his massive shoulder, tore the wood clear off its hinges. Zadie and I streamed into the room in his wake and processed the scene.

Lurch had one big hand around Mitch Rhoden's throat, the other holding a tight grip on the hand holding Mitch's gun. Stig Rhoden—dumb galoot he is—prepared to square up with Jaunty Hat. Stig still hadn't learned to set up a good guard, and Jaunty had just unsheathed the knife and brought it to the ready.

Behind them all, gaunt and almost unnoticed amid the fray, Captain Lance surveyed the chaos and tried to figure her way out. She noticed our entrance first, processed it without a blink, already scanning for an escape. "She's mine," I barked, but there was no need. Zadie Jayne flowed across the room and seized Jaunty Hat's knife hand, flashing a kick to Stig's stomach along the way. Big Wade crashed into Lurch and Mitch, taking them both down hard. It left me free to cross the room in three strides, swinging for Lance even as she brought her hands into a guard position. My fist crushed against her upper lip, left her spitting two teeth in the aftermath, and the following left broke her ribs and sapped her will to fight.

Lance fired back, jabbing sharp fingernails at my eyeballs and raking at my arms. It pissed me off, and a red mist settled over my vision. Lance barely stood a chance once I got my rage on, punches and pleading prove inefficient once I gave in to the berserker rage. I registered her strikes, each blow a distant explosion of light taking place somewhere beyond my immediate consciousness. I fired back with a wild haymaker, a crude punch owing less to skill and more to unrepressed anger. Lance jettisoned backwards, hitting the wall skull-first and with velocity, and the impact knocked her cold.

Zadie and Wade had already done their point, sweeping through the room like a destructive whirlwind and disarming potential weapons and narcotic injects. Zadie Jayne emptied Mitch's gun, jettisoning the ammunition and tucking the gun itself into her waistband. Jaunty Hat already lay sprawled on the floor, unconscious, with his hat rolling away from him, exposing its owner's growing bald spot.

Big Wade had Lurch down and sat upon him, using sheer weight to keep the big man contained.

Mitch Rhoden flattened herself against the wall, pale and nervous. She caught my eye, and clocked the anger there, letting loose a low-key whimper. "Please," she said. "I had no choice. These two were my cousin's friends. They accosted me, forced me to follow their plan to weaken you before your bout—"

"Stop," Zadie said. "We ain't buying it."

Mitch Rhoden fixed me with her wide, blue eyes. "But I promise it's the truth. I'm just a humble white harbor tea merchant—"

"Nah," I said. "You're not."

"I swear—"

"We were at the door," I said. "We heard everything."

Mitch Rhoden straightened her back and the innocent act fell away, replaced by a shrewd expression.

"It wasn't personal," she said. "Just a business proposition."

"Well, I took it personally," I said. "And it's unpleasant business."

Mitch sniffed and surveyed the carnage Zadie, Wade, and I unleashed. All her compatriots knocked out cold or trapped in Wade's sure grip. I locked my glare on her, already dreaming of knocking her block off.

She met my stare with poise and calm. "Let's resolve this like business people. You and your fellows have an exceptional talent for violence, as evidenced by your feats over the last few days. I'm fond of leaving such acts to third parties, although they're often idiots my cousin calls friends. How much has this all cost you?"

I glanced at Zadie, and she recited a number. Mitch Rhoden paled at the zeroes required, but she kept her cool. "I'll meet it," she said. "For your trouble."

Zadie's brows furrowed. "You've got the scratch?"

"I will," Mitch said, "one we put it about Lance called SecDiv in to cover the fact her man was done. I placed a few bets Valkyrie, on your advice, just to cover my tracks."

"You bet on me?"

"You're an impressive specimen," Mitch said, "and when you fought clear of the boys here, I figured there'd be a good chance you could take it all, despite our best efforts."

"What about her?" Zadie nudged the unconscious Lance with her foot.

"She'd led me into a dirty deal, and I don't appreciate it," Mitch Rhoden said. "I think it's best if Captain Lance left town and avoided White Harbor for a while."

"Very reasonable," I said.

"I'm a reasonable woman."

Zadie and I traded a quick look, and she nodded. "You can transfer the credits now?"

"Terminals in my pocket," Mitch said. "I'll need to get it out."

"Slowly," Zadie said.

I often think the world's divided into two major breeds: those who understand their limits, and those who don't. Captain Rackham accuses me of being the latter, but I've got a pretty good eye for just how much trouble I can handle, and it rarely steers me wrong.

Mitch Rhoden—much like her lunk-head cousin—didn't gauge the situation right. She got the draw open and tried to pull out a gun, a dinky little antique slug thrower. A hundred years out of style, but it had enough kick to be a threat. If she could have got it up and aimed, we might have been in ten kinds of trouble, but I don't fancy myself an idiot and Zadie Jayne is smarter than me, and we both expected a double-cross.

Maybe Mitch might have caught Big Wade, still focused on Lurch and lacking the sense to disable the big bastard, but Zadie and I moved in fluid unison as soon as Mitch tried to pull her arm out. My fist arced in, hard and angry, to hammer against Mitch Rhoden's ear. Zadie's hand snaked out and clubbed Mitch's arm, numbing nerves and breaking the grip on the weapon.

Mitch Rhoden staggered back, blinking like she'd just noticed something large and omnivorous in the room.

Then she slumped back into her office chair, head lolling to one side, blood and drool trickling down her face.

We turned on Lurch, Zadie and I, and offered him a choice. He dubbed speaking to SecDiv a far superior option to fighting me, Wade, and Zadie all at once. We took him down to the kitchen and stashed him in the lock-up, tying his hands and feet to the only wooden chair remaining after my escape.

Zadie gave him a dire warning against crossing us, then put in an anonymous tip to SecDiv as we high-tailed it back to the *Viking Maiden* in time to ship off on our next run. Captain Rackham met us at the airlock, raising one eyebrow in an unspoken query.

"Yeah," Zadie said. "It's done."

The airlock sealed behind us, the maglocks latching with a heavy thunk as the *Maiden* sealed up tight. Throughout the ship, the crew hustled, preparing for take-off.

Big Wade—breathing hard after the quick journey back—

screwed his face up and ventured his doubts. "You think SecDiv will prosecute without us there to make a statement?"

Captain Rackham fixed him with a bland stare and an idle, innocent grin. "I think they'll dig up something, now they know where to look for unsavory hi-jinx. I've got some old friends in SecDiv internal affairs, and they appreciated the heads up about a dirty Agent colluding with unsavory entities."

Wade blinked, not quite understanding, but he caught up as Zadie and I joined the Captain in a knowing grin. We don't know what Rackham did in the old days, before she took ownership of the *Maiden*, but the old woman knows some folks.

"Could live without a draw on my record," I said. "Grates my nerve to have Hockney out there thinking we're anything close to a fair and even fight."

The captain turned her stare on me.

"Word on the street says the fight wasn't finished, but there's footage of you knocking him out. *Someone* leaked it onto the local networks, and Majors decreed it your win on review. Local bookies aren't happy, but it's enough to keep us flying. And you're forgetting the important thing, Valkyrie."

"Oh, yeah?"

"Next time you're in the same port as Hockney, he'll be hankering for a rematch. Promotors across the sector will be eager to host and secure local streaming rights. Downside of being good, kid, people get used to the wins. An uncertainty makes folks eager to see a rematch, and there's always more money in the second fight if folks are hungry for it."

I rocked back on my heels as I worked through her logic, and it wasn't long before I was smiling.

ACKNOWLEDGMENTS

No writer produces work in a vacuum, but sometimes we wear our influences on our sleeve more obviously than others. I would note here the important inspiration for this story — Robert E. Howard's Sailor Steve Costigan stories — as well as the Robin Laws' writing on iconic and procedural heroes in fiction. Laws' *New Hero* anthologies and writing book changed the way I thought about character and narrative for the better.

I wrote the first Dana Valkyrie during the worst days of 2020 and 2021, when the shifting landscape of the pandemic meant I couldn't make progress on a novel about a darker, grimmer hero that I was meant to complete as part of my PhD on series fiction. Dana seemed like a protagonist who would be fun, and I desperately needed fun in my life at the time. My thanks go out to my supervisors, Kim Wilkins and Natalie Collie, who provided important feedback on early drafts.

Thanks also go out to the all folks who backed the Eclectic Projects Patreon during its three-year existence. Some read an early iteration of this story and provided much-needed encouragement, but all created a safe space to try doing something out of my comfort zone as a writer. Thank you to Margaret Ball, Kate Eltham, Nicole Strickland, Jodi, Meg Vann, Sally Ball, Jennifer White, Maggie Slater, David Versace, Mark Webb, Seagoat, Kathleen Jennings, Kylie Scott, Tansy Rayner Roberts, Lois Spangler, Ben Francisco, Anja Peerdeman, Trent Jamieson, Catherine Caine, and Stephanie Gunn.

A special thanks to my wife, Sarah "Zazz" Hobday, and Team Write Club: Angela Slatter, Kathleen Jennings, and Joanne Anderton. My thanks also go out to the Sunday Night Cthulhu Crew of Allan Carey, Nicola Logan, Nic Holland, and Adam

Norris, who have listen to me bang on about the pulp publishing era and pulp writers so often there has surely been 1d3 SAN loss somewhere along the line.

ABOUT THE AUTHOR

PETER M. BALL is an author, publisher, and RPG gamer whose love of speculative fiction emerged after exposure to *The Hobbit*, *Star Wars*, David Lynch's *Dune*, and far too many games of *Dungeons and Dragons* before the age of 7. He's spent the bulk of his life working as a creative writing tutor, with brief stints as a performance poet, gaming convention organizer, online content developer, non-profit arts manager, project manager, GenreCon convener, and d20 RPG publisher.

He's the author of the Miriam Aster series and the Keith Murphy Urban Fantasy Thrillers, three short story collections, and more stories, articles, poems, and RPG material than he'd care to count. He's returning to Eclectic Projects magazine after a short hiatus devoted to finishing his Doctorate with the University of Queensland.

In 2017, Peter founded Brain Jar Press to publish his backlist. From 2020, Brain Jar Press has grown to become one of Australia's finest micro presses publishing new and reprint fantasy, science fiction, horror, and crime work, with a catalogue including some some of the finest speculative fiction and crime writers working in Australia and beyond.

Peter's work has won Aurealis Awards, Dither Awards, and has appeared in Years Best compilations. He's an aspiring mad scientist running publishing and genre experiments through the Eclectic Projects imprint, and resides in Brisbane, Australia, with his partner and two cats. There's a very good chance he's in need of coffee right now.

Find Peter Online at PeterMBall.com or reach out to Peter on your favorite Social Media platforms:

facebook.com / PeterMBall

instagram.com / PeterMBall

goodreads.com / PeterMBall

threads.net / @PeterMBall

bookbub.com / authors / peter-m-ball

ALSO BY PETER M. BALL

SHORT STORY COLLECTIONS

The Birdcage Heart & Other Strange Tales

Not Quite The End Of the World Just Yet: Short Stories & Strange Futures

These Strange & Magic Things: Short Stories

Unfamiliar Shores: Short Stories

KEITH MURPHY URBAN FANTASY THRILLERS

Exile

Frost

Crusade

Local Heroes

Gold Coast Ragnarok (Omnibus)

MIRIAM ASTER NOVELLAS

Horn

Bleed

Unicorns, Fey, and a Hardboiled Dame (Omnibus)

ESSAYS

You Don't Want To Be Published & Other Things Nobody Tells You When You First Start Writing

CHAPBOOKS

Deeper Cuts: Night, Morning, Story & Impact

Gold Coast, 2002: Poems

NEWSLETTER SIGN-UP

Be the first to know!

Sign up for the Peter M. Ball newsletter to and you'll get the latest news on releases and deals, plus an ebook starter library and the occasional give away.

What are you waiting for? Sign up at

petermball.com/newsletter.